# MILL TOWN NURSE

When nurse Lucy Hirst leaves a London hospital to take charge of the First Aid department at Earnshaw Mill in Lenthwaite, she found that she had not left the drama of a big hospital behind. For two men come into her life—Mike Earnshaw, son of the mill's owner, and Alan Tolson, the local doctor with whom she works at the mill—and, as ever, the course of love is anything but smooth . . .

# MILL
# TOWN
# NURSE

## Lilian Woodward

**ATLANTIC LARGE PRINT**
Chivers Press, Bath, England.
Curley Publishing, Inc.,
South Yarmouth, Mass., USA.

**Library of Congress Cataloging-in-Publication Data**

Woodward, Lilian.
  Mill town nurse / Lilian Woodward.
    p.  cm.—(Atlantic large print)
  ISBN 0–7927–0219–0
  1. Large type books.  I. Title
[PR6073.0635M55  1990]
823′.914—dc20
                                 90–30462
                                    CIP

**British Library Cataloguing in Publication Data**

Woodward, Lilian, *1907–*
  Mill town nurse.
  I. Title
  823.912 [F]
  ISBN 0–7451–9783–3
  ISBN 0–7451–9795–7 pbk

This Large Print edition is published by Chivers Press, England, and
Curley Publishing, Inc, U.S.A. 1990

Published by arrangement with the author

U.K. Hardback ISBN 0 7451 9783 3
U.K. Softback ISBN 0 7451 9795 7
U.S.A. Softback ISBN 0 7927 0219 0

# MILL TOWN NURSE

# PART ONE

# LENTHWAITE

## CHAPTER ONE

As the train ran into the station Lucy Hirst lowered the window and looked eagerly out of the compartment.

Then she smiled with pleasure.

For there, looking along the train, was the large dependable figure of her brother, Dick. She waved. Seeing her, he waved back and hurried towards her.

'Lucy!' He gave her a quick hug.

'Dick! Thanks for coming to meet me!'

He took her suitcase and they walked towards the barrier where Lucy gave up her ticket.

'How's Mum—and Dad?' Lucy demanded and Dick's plain good-natured face grinned back at her.

'You'll know soon enough,' he declared, and as they crossed the station yard: 'What do you think about this?'

'This' was a small car parked in the car park. It was an old Mini polished till it shone. It was obviously the pride of Dick Hirst's heart.

1

'My word, we are going up in the world!' Lucy smiled. 'When did you buy it?'

'Last week-end.'

He put her case in the back and she slipped into the passenger seat.

As they drove out of the station Lucy looked about her.

Dear little Lenthwaite! It hadn't changed a scrap since she had gone to London four years ago as a student nurse to St. Christopher's Hospital in the East End.

She had returned from time to time to Yorkshire to see her parents; but as the work in the understaffed hospital increased, and she had to give more and more time to studying for her exams, her visits had been fewer than she would have liked.

But now she was fully qualified and was eagerly anticipating this holiday—ten days of freedom—in the small town where she had been born twenty-three years before.

The little car drove along the narrow main street with, at the far end, the towering mass of Earnshaw's Mill. The heavy iron gates were closed for it was half-past five and the mill workers had gone home an hour before.

Away beyond the mill a hill rose to the moors which surrounded the little mill town, heather clad moors on which Lucy, as a child, had played and walked so often.

Dick drove past the mill then turned into a terrace of neat little houses built of the local

2

stone. Half-way along he stopped outside a newly painted house with spotless curtains hanging at the windows and the front step scrubbed almost white.

As the car drew up the front door was thrown open and a woman looked out. Her thin face under her greying hair was shining with joy. She held out her arms to Lucy who, jumping from the car, ran towards her.

'Mum!'

'Oh, Lucy lass, it's good to see you! It must be six months since you were last home.'

Lucy kissed her mother. Arms about each other, they went into the little house, Dick following with his sister's suitcase.

'Where's Dad?' Lucy asked as they went along the narrow hallway towards the open door of the kitchen.

'Here I am, lass!' Sam Hirst was standing beside the table which was laid for tea.

He kissed his daughter warmly. He was a big broad-shouldered man with kindly brown eyes in a square good-natured face. There was hardly any grey in his plentiful black hair. He had come in from the mill only a few minutes before and he was still in his working clothes.

'Better get changed, Sam!' his wife said sharply. 'I'll be putting the tea on the table in a quarter of an hour and we don't want to find ourselves waiting for you!'

Mr. Hirst winked at Lucy and turned to the door. They heard his heavy tread as he

3

went upstairs. Dick, who had taken his sister's case up to her room, came into the kitchen.

Lucy, not for the first time, noticed how different her brother's appearance was from her father's. Both worked at the big Earnshaw mill, which employed about a fifth of the adult population of Lenthwaite; but whereas Mr. Hirst was only an overlooker in charge of one of the weaving sheds, Dick had early shown his qualities as a designer and was now a responsible member of the team which designed Earnshaw cloth, which was exported to nearly every country in the world.

'Not married yet, then, Dick?' she asked as her mother made for the cooker to turn the chops which, a few minutes earlier, she had put under the grill.

He grinned. 'No, and not likely to be!'

'I should think Bessie's growing tired of waiting for you to ask her.'

A sudden frown banished the smile.

'Why everyone thinks that just because Bessie and I have grown up together I should marry her, I'll never know,' he grunted.

'Sorry I spoke!' Lucy laughed, then looking at her mother: 'I'll just go up and have a wash then take some things out of my case.'

'All right, love! Tea won't be ready for ten minutes or so.'

Lucy went up the narrow stairs to the

4

landing above. Four doors opened off this. Three were bedrooms, the other a bathroom.

Lucy could hear her father in the bathroom so she went into her room. It was as it had always been. Ever since she went to London it had stood waiting for her to come home. She felt to be returning to her childhood whenever she went into the little room with its sprigged wallpaper, its single bed with the red bed-spread and the rather flimsy wardrobe and dressing table.

She looked into the dressing table mirror. She saw a slim dark-haired girl with wide-set hazel eyes. She smiled at her rather serious face and the solemn expression vanished. Suddenly she laughed outright remembering how a patient had once said: 'You look as if butter wouldn't melt in your mouth, nurse. But that's a firm little chin you've got! I daresay you're a wilful madam when you're roused!'

She went to the window and looked across the narrow street to the houses on the other side.

Exactly opposite No. 24 Harper Street—her father's house—was the house in which the Shaw family lived. Bessie Shaw had been her best friend since they had attended the local infants' school together. Their friendship had not ended when she had gone to the big London hospital. They had exchanged letters regularly and Lucy knew all

5

about her friend's job as private secretary to Mr. Earnshaw, Chairman and Managing Director of Matthew Earnshaw and Co. Ltd, Worsted Manufacturers.

She opened her suitcase and hung the dresses she had brought with her in the little wardrobe, then, hearing her father come out of the bathroom, she went along to wash then went downstairs again.

It was a happy meal.

Lucy, snatching a hurried snack in the hospital canteen, had often thought in the last few years of the homely kitchen with her mother carrying the heaped plates direct from the cooker to the table, and her father and Dick tucking in 'as if they hadn't seen food for a fortnight', as her mother often said.

'We haven't congratulated you yet on passing your final exams, lass,' Sam said, smiling across the table at Lucy. 'I reckon nothing can stop you now. Sister next, then Matron, eh?'

'They don't call them matrons any more, Dad!' Lucy smiled. 'Not that I've any ambition to be a Senior Nursing Officer—or even a Sister. I'm quite happy being a common or garden SRN.'

'I hear Nurse Bailey's going to retire,' Dick put in.

His mother looked at him sharply.

'Nay, never! She's quite a fixture at Earnshaw's.'

'She's been in charge of the First Aid department for thirty years. She probably thinks she's earned a rest,' Mr. Hirst said conveying a well-loaded fork to his mouth.

His wife looked at Lucy.

'How about it, love? They'll need someone if Maggie Bailey goes.'

Lucy met her mother's blue eyes. There was something wistful in the older woman's expression. She knew exactly what her mother was thinking.

Ever since she had gone to London she had been aware that her mother missed her dreadfully; and from the hints that her father and Dick had dropped in their letters, Mrs. Hirst was not too well, though her mother would never have allowed herself to admit any such thing.

'I hardly think it's my sort of job, Mum,' she murmured.

'It's important work,' her father said. 'Oh, I know that dressing the cuts and bruises of a lot of mill workers isn't as important as work in a big London hospital, but—well, it has to be done by someone.'

'Dr. Tolson called to see me yesterday,' Mrs. Hirst said, and seeing Lucy's frown, she added hastily: 'Oh, it was nothing, love. Just my rheumatism playing me up again. He was saying how highly he thinks of Nurse Bailey. He and she must make a wonderful team.'

'I didn't know he was the mill doctor,'

Lucy exclaimed.

'Yes, he took over when old Dr. Bancroft died. It's only a part-time appointment, of course. I don't think you've met him yet, have you love?'

'No! Do you like him as much as Dr. Bancroft?'

'Yes! I didn't think I'd get used to having a much younger man looking after us all, but—well, he's so kind and understanding. I can't help liking him. He's never in a hurry. Always ready for a little chat.'

She cut up a large apple pie and Lucy handed the plates round. A jugful of thick cream went from hand to hand as Mrs. Hirst produced a big teapot and poured four large cups of tea.

Lucy felt a thrill of happiness. How wonderful it was to be home enjoying a Yorkshire High Tea once again! When she had first gone to London it had taken her several months to get used to the different eating habits of people in the south.

It flashed across her mind that it would be rather fun to return to Lenthwaite to live and work. She had never enjoyed London, though she had loved her work at the big hospital.

She heard the street door open and a voice she instantly recognised calling 'Coo-ee!'

'It's Bessie!' she cried, jumping up and running out into the hall to greet her friend.

The two girls flew into each other's arms.

8

'Oh, Lucy, let me look at you!' Bessie cried, and held her friend at arm's length.

She was a tall girl with fair curly hair and twinkling blue eyes. Her soft red lips always seemed to be trembling on the brink of laughter. Her lively face escaped real prettiness because of the short turned-up little nose which she always said God had put on as an after thought just before she was born.

'How long are you staying?' she demanded now as they went into the kitchen together.

'Till a week next Tuesday,' Lucy replied.

'Good! I'll be able to see lots of you.' She grinned at Dick. 'I saw that old boneshaker of yours draw up so I knew she'd arrived.'

'Have a cup of tea, Bessie!' Mrs. Hirst invited.

'No, thanks! I promised Mum I'd only be a minute so that I could welcome the prodigal daughter. But don't let me interrupt your meal.'

'We were talking about Nurse Bailey leaving Earnshaw's,' Mrs. Hirst said.

'Yes! She gave her notice in two days ago. I saw her when she came to speak to Mr. Earnshaw. She didn't seem to want to leave, but her sister—who lives in Devon—wants her to go and live with her and she decided the time had come for her to pack the job in. She's been at Earnshaw's for thirty-two years. She'll be sixty in a month's time.'

'You must try and persuade our Lucy to

apply for the job!' Sam Hirst said, stirring his tea.

'Oh, if only she would!' Bessie cried, eyes shining. 'I think she'd get the job, too. There won't be a real rush of applicants to come to Lenthwaite, I'm sure!'

Lucy laughed. 'What makes you think I would rush to take a job in Lenthwaite?'

'Well, of course, having tasted the joys of life in the south, you might think Lenthwaite was very small fry,' Dick put in drily. 'If I were you, Sis, I'd finish what you started. You'll never become a—a—what did you call it?—a Senior Nursing Officer in a small West Riding mill town, certainly not at Matthew Earnshaw and Company Limited.'

'I must fly!' Bessie said, effectively ending the discussion. 'I'll come across later, if I may, Lucy. There's such a lot to talk about.'

After Mr. Hirst had gone to feed his pigeons in the yard at the back of the little house, and Dick had taken his car to the local garage for petrol, Lucy and her mother washed up.

It was cosy in the warm little kitchen with the fire sparkling on the copper pans and the curtains drawn against the early spring evening. Mrs. Hirst sighed. Lucy looked at her anxiously.

'Are you all right, Mum?' she asked, and when her mother frowned: 'Oh, I know you'll never talk about yourself, but—well, you

10

don't look as well as you looked when I saw you last.'

Mrs. Hirst bit her lip. She looked into Lucy's face.

'I'll admit it, lass,' she said quietly. 'I keep it from your father and Dick but—well, no I'm not a hundred per cent, I must agree.'

'What does Dr. Tolson say?'

'He won't commit himself. He's treating me for rheumatism and I must say he's eased the pain a great deal lately.' Her eyes softened. 'Eee, lass, if only you could come back to Lenthwaite. Sometimes I feel I don't have a daughter any more with you being so far away.'

'I'm sorry, Mum,' Lucy whispered and gave her mother a sudden tight hug.

'It's selfish of me to talk like that,' Mrs. Hirst said. 'Forget I said anything, love. You have your own life to live. You've a fine career before you.'

When Lucy did not speak she looked at her closely.

'Haven't you got a boy friend?' she asked. 'You're a pretty girl. Surely one of those doctors at that hospital of yours should have become interested in you by now.'

Lucy shook her head.

'There's nobody—any more,' she said in a low voice. 'There was—once. But—he's marrying someone else.'

Mrs. Hirst wiped her hands.

'Was he the one you mentioned once or twice in your letters?'

'Yes, Mum, Geoffrey Baines. He's obviously going to do big things as a surgeon—when he settles down. He's marrying the daughter of a consultant. He was on her father's firm at the hospital. Sir Henry Filson.'

Mrs. Hirst cried angrily: 'He'd no right to throw you over like that, just to further his career.'

'Oh, I don't think it was only that, Mum. Ruth Filson's a very attractive girl. And Geoffrey and I were only friends.'

Yet even as she spoke she felt once again the stab of pain that had pierced her when she had first heard, from one of the other nurses, that Geoffrey's engagement had been announced in that morning's newspaper.

Until that day she had been happy at St. Christopher's, loved her work on the wards, enjoyed the many friendships she had made.

But when she no longer had Geoffrey to go around with—gay, mad-cap, lovable Geoffrey—things had been very flat. She had turned to her studies with even greater intensity, had hardly left the precincts of the hospital buildings.

'He made you unhappy, didn't he, love?' Mrs. Hirst said, pressing Lucy's hand.

Lucy smiled brightly. 'Of course not, Mum. It was just one of those things. I was

12

fond of him—yes!—but he never led me on to expect anything more than friendship.'

The door bell rang. Mrs. Hirst frowned.

'Now who can this be?' she exclaimed.

'I'll go!' Lucy said and made for the door. Mrs. Hirst looked in the mirror and patted her grey hair into place.

'Yes, love. It could be the insurance man though he usually comes on Thursdays.'

Lucy went down the dark hall and opened the front door. A man was standing outside. He was about thirty and had a lean rather drawn face. His grey eyes inspected Lucy for a moment before he spoke.

'Is Mrs. Hirst in?' he asked, then added: 'I'm Dr. Tolson. I happened to be passing and thought I'd just take a look at her.'

'Please come in,' Lucy invited, and as he walked into the house: 'I'm Lucy Hirst. I've just come home from London.'

He smiled at her, a smile which lit up his rather solemn face.

'I'm so glad to meet you, Miss Hirst,' he said. 'Your mother has told me so much about you.'

He made for the kitchen as if he had been that way often before. Lucy followed and heard him greet her mother.

'How are you feeling tonight, Mrs. Hirst?'

'Much better, thank you, doctor.' His patient was rather flustered. 'This is my daughter. She's just arrived back from

13

London.'

'Yes, we've met,' he smiled with a glance at Lucy. 'Your mother tells me you passed your Finals. Congratulations!'

'Thank you!' She turned away. 'I'll just go up and unpack.'

She went upstairs. She liked the look of Dr. Tolson. He seemed capable and competent. She was relieved that her mother's health was in such able hands.

Her room was at the back and as she finished unpacking she could hear the murmur of voices below. When these ceased she went to the top of the stairs. Dr. Tolson was letting himself out. She ran lightly down and stood with him on the pavement outside the house for a few moments.

'How is my mother?' she asked.

He did not speak for a few seconds then he looked into her face.

'Not as well as I would like to see her,' he said quietly. 'I'm sure she'll be much happier to have you at home for a while. She works much too hard for a woman in her condition.'

'I shall help her all I can while I'm at home,' she said.

He allowed himself a thin smile.

'And when you go away again?'

'We must work something out,' she murmured feeling suddenly angry at the hidden criticism in the young doctor's words.

'I hope so! Goodnight, Miss Hirst!'

14

He went round the car and seated himself at the wheel. She watched him turn in the narrow street then drive away until the red tail light disappeared round the corner into the main road; then she went thoughtfully back into the house.

## CHAPTER TWO

The following afternoon Lucy took the well-remembered track through the heather to the top of the moor.

It was a warm sunny day for early April. White clouds chased each other across the blue sky and the breeze stirred the heather as it swept down from the ridge above.

Tiring of the long climb Lucy turned to look back the way she had come.

Lenthwaite lay below her in the valley, a huddle of houses overshadowed by the two great mills which employed most of its people.

Immediately below her was Earnshaw's Mill, at the other side of the town Murgatroyd's. Both had high chimneys which seemed like strict fingers demanding the attention of the other.

There were other little mills and factories but these were very small fry in comparison with their enormous neighbours.

15

As Lucy turned to continue her climb she remembered how, over the years, she had heard tales of the rivalry there had always been between the Earnshaws and the Murgatroyds. It went back more than a hundred years when the two businesses had been founded by the grandfathers of the present owners.

Now old Mr. Murgatroyd was dead. Her mother had told her six months before that he had passed away and that his daughter, Rosalind—he had no son—was running the business.

Lucy had seen Rosalind Murgatroyd several times before she had gone to London. Usually Rosalind was sitting at the wheel of a car, either shopping in the little town or driving along the road to Leeds to visit the shops in the big Yorkshire city.

Rosalind, as Lucy remembered her, was a thin pretty girl with fair hair. She was said to be like her mother who had died when she was a little girl.

As she reached the top of the long slope Lucy wondered how Rosalind would handle the complex affairs of a business like Murgatroyd's. Apparently she had a manager so presumably she would leave the day to day running of the mill to him. But the final decision on important matters would be hers. How would she face up to her responsibilities?

But Lucy forgot Rosalind Murgatroyd as she strode across the moor. Now she was out of sight of Lenthwaite. Only the vastness of the moor surrounded her.

Up here there were only the moorland sheep and the peewits who wheeled and cried over her head. There was no track and she walked carefully knowing how easy it would be to turn her ankle and find herself with a long painful limp home.

She threw back her head and drew in great breaths of the heady moorland air. How different it was from the flat used-up London air which she had breathed for so many months since her last visit to Yorkshire.

She thought of London and wondered whether she wanted to go back to St. Christopher's and the sudden emptiness of her life there now that Geoffrey was to marry someone else.

'But I must go back!' she told herself fiercely. 'It's my job. It's what I was trained for.'

She strode on, her thoughts on the past then on the future. She had been so happy. Would she be as happy when Geoffrey was married and had gone out of her life for ever?

She did not notice that clouds had spread in over the moor from the west. The blue sky had vanished. The breeze, which earlier had refreshed her, had now turned colder and was finding its way through the jacket of the suit she was wearing.

Then she felt a few spots of rain on her face. Her heart sank. She was in for a soaking!

She climbed another ridge and saw that a curtain of rain was driving towards her from Lancashire. From this point she should have been able to see the tall chimneys of the cotton towns some ten miles away.

But these were hidden in the rain and she knew that she must return home without delay.

She turned up the collar of her jacket. She could only hope that the rain clouds did not settle on the moor as they sometimes did.

The few spots of rain had now turned into a deluge. She started to run. She had a good sense of direction and she knew that if she kept on her present course she would, in about half an hour, come to the top of the slope up which she had climbed earlier.

She heard a sudden noise behind her. It was the heavy beat of an engine and at first she stood, puzzled, looking round. Surely there could not be a motor car up here. Even a tractor was unlikely.

But the noise was increasing and suddenly she realised that it was overhead.

She peered upwards but without seeing anything.

It must be an aeroplane flying through the clouds, she decided, as she once again went

18

on her way.

But the droning sound increased and once more she looked round.

Then suddenly she saw it, a small machine with whirling blades. It was almost overhead.

She could even see the figure of a man at the controls inside the perspex cabin. ,

It was a small helicopter and it was hovering right over her.

As she watched the little machine sank to the moor. A moment later it was stationary and the engine fell silent as the blades ceased to revolve.

A man climbed from the tiny cabin and made towards her.

He was about twenty-five, she decided, and he was powerfully built with dark unruly hair and twinkling brown eyes.

'Can I give you a lift?' he asked and his white teeth flashed in a smile, and when she hesitated: 'I'm going to Lenthwaite. It might be a good idea if you come with me. I don't suppose you want to get soaked to the skin!'

What a fright I must look! she thought. Already she could feel the rain running off the end of her nose. She dare not think what her hair must look like. She must resemble a drowned rat!

'But I—' she began, not knowing quite what to say.

She might have accepted a lift in a car. But in a helicopter! She had never heard of such a thing before.

'Well, make up your mind!' he said rather impatiently. 'Even if you want a soaking I don't!'

'All right!' Suddenly she made up her mind.

'Good girl!' He took her arm and urged her towards the machine a dozen yards away. 'I'm Mike Earnshaw, by the way!'

So that's who he was! She had thought there was something familiar about him. She should have recognised him earlier. After all, his father employed her own father and brother!

'I'm Lucy Hirst,' she said, but he said nothing to this for now they had reached the little machine and he had opened the cabin door and was telling her to scramble in.

She found no difficulty in climbing into the passenger seat. Mike Earnshaw got behind the controls. He grinned at her as he switched on the engine. The blades overhead started to turn then, with a roar, they came to full power.

'Up we go!' the young man murmured and, like a lift ascending, the helicopter swooped up from the moor like an ungainly bird.

'I haven't seen you about Lenthwaite before,' Mike Earnshaw said as they flew over the moor.

'I've been in London for the past four years,' she said.

'You're visiting someone in Lenthwaite, are you?'

She laughed. 'No, my home's there. As a matter of fact, if you're Mr. Earnshaw of Earnshaw Mill, my father and brother both work for you.'

'Hirst!' he said. 'Why, you must be Sam Hirst's daughter. And of course, Dick Hirst's in our design department.'

'Right first time!'

'What do you do in London, Miss Hirst?'

'I'm a nurse at St. Christopher's Hospital in Limehouse.'

'A nurse, eh? Now I come to think of it my father's secretary, Miss Shaw, mentioned something about a friend who was a nurse. It must have been you.'

'It was. Bessie and I have been friends since we were at school together.'

They came low over the ridge and there below lay Lenthwaite.

'I shall have to land on the pad at the Manor,' Mike said. 'I'll run you home in my car.'

They flew over the little town and Lucy, looking out of the tiny cabin, saw several faces turned up to watch them.

Beyond the town stood a large house in extensive grounds. The helicopter hovered over this for a few seconds then settled gently to a cleared space near an ornamental lake.

Presently they were safely down. Mike

switched off the engine then jumped out of the cabin and ran round to help Lucy to the ground.

'You must come in for a drink and to get dry,' he said.

'I really ought to be getting home,' she said.

'I'll run you home later,' he said, and before she could say any more he turned to a man who was running towards them across the grass: 'Look after my things, Barnes.'

The man nodded. Mike took Lucy's arm.

'We'll go to the house and have a glass of sherry while your jacket dries.'

She sighed. This was a masterful young man, indeed.

Leaving the mechanic to secure the helicopter they walked across the grass to the big house. It was a massive affair and was typical of the mansions the first rich woollen manufacturers had built at the end of the last century. It had high twisted chimneys, a number of gables and narrow windows set in thick stone walls.

'Hideous, isn't it?' Mike laughed and the colour came to Lucy's cheeks knowing he had seen her expression. 'It's stuffy in summer and cold in winter, in spite of central heating. But it suits my father. I suppose it does something for his ego. The big mill boss. Looked up to by all! He little knows!'

There was something in his voice which

made Lucy glance at him. He seemed almost bitter as if thinking of his father gave him no pleasure.

They reached the big portico which sheltered the front door. Mike opened this and ushered Lucy into a large hall. A wide staircase rose from this to a gallery off which opened several rooms.

A big fire burned in an enormous fireplace in the hall. On a table at the foot of the staircase was a flower arrangement of carnations and roses. On the panelled walls hung half a dozen oil paintings, mostly landscapes, though one was of a bearded man standing in a stiff pose, a book in his hand.

'My grandfather, Matthew Earnshaw,' Mike said, following Lucy's glance. 'Founded the business when he was selling cloth in Bradford market. Borrowed money to get started, and with a great deal of self-confidence and not a little trickery, made the Earnshaw name famous throughout the West Riding.'

'Really, Mike, that's not fair!'

Lucy looked round. The voice had come from the other side of the hall. A door had opened and a woman was standing looking across at Mike and herself.

'Hullo, Mother!' Mike said. 'This is Lucy Hirst. I saved her from a fate worse than death on the moor when the rain started. She's come to get dry and have a drink.'

The woman, who had a round pleasant face under dark beautifully dressed hair, smiled. She was wearing a well-cut tweed suit.

'Perhaps she'd like to go in the cloakroom first,' she said, and nodded towards a door across the hall. 'Come in the sitting room when you're ready, my dear.'

Lucy was glad to escape. In the cloakroom she dried her hair on a towel and applied some make-up. Then she went to join the others. Mike was standing in the doorway of a room in which a large fire was blazing.

It was the most cheerful feature of the big room, which was filled with bulky pieces of furniture which did not seem too comfortable to Lucy. More rather dull landscapes hung on the dark walls.

'Here she is, Mother!' Mike said, escorting her into the room.

Mrs. Earnshaw was standing with her back to the fire. She smiled at the visitor.

'What will you have to drink, dear?' she asked. 'I'll get it for you while Mike takes your jacket to the kitchen to be dried.'

'My jacket's only damp,' Lucy said. 'There's really no reason to dry it.'

'Then take it off and I'll hang it in front of this fire while you have your drink,' Mrs. Earnshaw suggested.

Though Mike's mother was friendly enough Lucy was conscious of being examined carefully. No doubt Mrs. Earnshaw was wondering who she was, did she live locally, who her parents were.

'Lucy's father and brother work at the mill,' Mike said as he pulled up a chair and hung Lucy's jacket over it before the fire.

'Indeed!' Mrs. Earnshaw said and though the smile was still there Lucy detected a faint touch of frost in the quiet voice.

'Do you work at—Earnshaw's?' the older woman asked after a slight pause.

Lucy smiled. 'No, I'm a nurse in London.'

'A nurse! That's a very good thing to be!' Mrs. Earnshaw's voice was warmer now. 'Do you like the work?'

'I love it!'

'Do you often visit Lenthwaite?'

'Not as much as I'd like to do. As a matter of fact, I've been pretty busy lately with my exams. I took my Finals just before I came home.'

'And did you pass?' Mike asked, handing her a glass.

'I'm glad to say I did. I'm fully qualified now.'

'Good for you!' Mike cried, then asked her about the hospital and her life in London. But when he wanted her to have another sherry she shook her head.

'No, thank you. I must be getting home. My mother will be growing anxious.'

He tried to persuade her to stay longer but she was adamant.

'Then I'll run you home,' he said.

He helped her into her jacket. Mrs. Earnshaw held out her hand. Lucy took it. It was soft and fragile in her own warm grasp.

'Goodbye, my dear,' the older woman said. 'It's been nice meeting you.'

'Thank you for the drink,' Lucy said.

As she followed Mike into the hall she had the feeling that as soon as the door closed behind her Mrs. Earnshaw would forget all about her.

Mike's car was an expensive foreign model. Lucy, sinking into the passenger seat, wondered what it must be like to be surrounded on all sides by luxury as the Earnshaws were. Perhaps one would get tired of it after a time, she mused.

Mike drove the car at a fast speed down the winding drive to the main road.

'Can I see you again?' he asked, his eyes on the road again.

She frowned. Did she want to see him again? She liked him, but was it wise to get too friendly with handsome young men who exuded charm out of every pore? She had had one experience of that already.

'I don't think perhaps it would be wise,' she murmured.

'Why ever not! There's little enough to do in this god-forsaken place. You're different. You're like a breath of fresh air blowing from the south.'

'The air isn't all that fresh where I come from,' she laughed. 'In fact, the air of Limehouse is stale and used up.'

He scowled. 'You know what I mean! Surely we could have a meal together. There are one or two reasonable restaurants around Lenthwaite.'

'I'll see,' she compromised; then as they passed the Earnshaw Mill: 'I live down the next turning. Number twenty-four.'

He drew up outside Lucy's home. She stepped out.

'Thanks for bringing me home, Mr. Earnshaw,' she said.

He gave her a mock salute.

'It was my pleasure,' he said, then: 'You'll be hearing from me.'

Before she could reply he revved up the engine, did a U-turn and raced off towards the main road again.

Lucy, with a sigh, opened the door of the house and made for the kitchen.

'Who was making all that noise outside?' her mother demanded, turning from the stove.

'A young man called Earnshaw,' Lucy said. 'He picked me up in—in his helicopter and took me to the Manor for a drink. And now he's just brought me home in his sports car.'

Her mother's mouth fell open.

'Pull the other one. It's got bells on,' she said, unbelieving, but Lucy only smiled, turned and made for the stairs.

She felt she wanted to be alone to think over the events of the last hour.

## CHAPTER THREE

Mr. Earnshaw was a big balding man with piercing slate-coloured eyes and a tight mouth that plainly told the world that he did not tolerate fools, or indeed anyone who disagreed with him. Respected but not liked by customers and competitors, he was yet regarded as one of the shrewdest businessmen in the West Riding.

'No one gets the better of Matthew Earnshaw,' was one of his favourite sayings, and indeed for the most part he was right.

There was only one fly in the ointment as far as he was concerned.

Rosalind Murgatroyd.

And, to a lesser degree, his son, Mike.

On the day following Mike's meeting with Lucy, the two men confronted each other in Mr. Earnshaw's office at the mill.

It was a gloomy room with dark panelling, heavy furniture and an uncurtained window that looked out on the mill yard.

Mr. Earnshaw's eyes were blazing angrily.

'But how long do you think that girl is going to wait for you to ask her to marry you!'

he shouted, his face crimson with rage.

Mike lit a cigarette and blew the smoke towards the ceiling.

'Why are you so sure that Rosalind would be prepared to marry me?' he asked. 'She must know very well that all you want is to take over the Murgatroyd Mill and that the easiest way of doing that is for her to marry me.'

'If her father hadn't died when he did he'd have come to an arrangement with me about combining the two businesses,' Mr. Earnshaw said.

'I doubt it! You know as well as I know, Dad, that he hated you as much as you hated him!'

His father snorted ferociously.

'Just because we were keen competitors doesn't mean we hated each other. I pointed out to him many times that as our processes of manufacture were much the same we could save a lot of money by amalgamating. But he'd never listen to me.'

'You know very well that the terms you put to him meant you would be the boss and he'd be very much your second in command. Henry Murgatroyd was a proud man. He wouldn't have stomached such an arrangement.'

His father stamped angrily over to the window and glared out into the mill yard. A passing workman, meeting his eye, hurried towards the nearest door as if afraid that at any moment his employer's wrathful voice might demand an explanation as to why he was in the mill yard, and not in the weaving shed.

'We're not concerned with Henry Murgatroyd any more,' Mr. Earnshaw declared. 'Rosalind's been in love with you since she was a little girl, and I've always thought you had a soft spot for her in your heart, lad.'

He turned from the window. There was a kinder expression on his face now.

'I really have your happiness at heart, Mike,' he said. 'You must know that. Rosalind Murgatroyd would make the perfect wife for you, and if it brought two great businesses together—well, that would be to the advantage of all.'

Mike frowned. He stubbed out his cigarette in the big ashtray which Matthew Earnshaw used when he smoked a cigar. His father frowned irritably but did not scold him.

'I do like Rosalind, Dad,' Mike said. 'It's just that—well, I don't love her. We grew up together, that's all.'

'Love!' His father seemed on the point of losing his temper again. 'Every Tom, Dick and Harry seems to think that love matters more than anything else. It doesn't lad, and you'll find that out in time. Look at your mother and me. I married her and she brought some money into the business when we were going through a bad patch. But if I'd stopped to think "Do I love her!" we'd never have married and where would we be now?'

'Poor Mother!' Mike muttered feelingly. His father scowled at him.

'We've been happy enough as I'm sure your mother will agree, just as you and Rosalind would be happy if you hadn't got this daft idea about love in your head.' He walked back to his chair behind the big desk and sank into it. 'Anyhow, think on, Mike. I expect you to ask Rosalind to name the day, and the sooner the better. I've put up with your idling about ever since you left that university your mother insisted on sending you to, but I won't put up with it much more. If you don't do as I say a big change might be coming in your life, my lad. And the change won't include helicopters and sports cars and all that go with them.'

He picked up some papers from the desk and started to study them. Mike, after standing there for a few seconds more, turned on his heel and went into the outer office.

Bessie Shaw, seated at her typewriter, smiled sympathetically at him as he passed. She'd probably heard the row, Mike thought, and bit his lip angrily. It never seemed to occur to his father to keep private discussion for home. He always had to shout at the top of his voice about the most intimate matters

31

so that everybody on the premises could hear him.

He left the mill. He was supposed to go to his desk in the accounts office which his father, several months before, had decreed he should occupy until such time as he was moved to another department in the mill.

This process was known as 'learning the business', and Mike hated it. His only interest in the business was in selling the cloth its workers produced. More than once he had asked his father to send him out 'on the road' to persuade merchants to buy Earnshaw cloth.

'You're not ready for that side of things yet,' Mr. Earnshaw had told him brusquely and had banished him to the accounts office for six months.

Mike got into his car and drove into the town. He wanted to go to his bank for some money, then he meant to have a cup of coffee in the little town's only coffee shop.

Leaving the bank he met Rosalind Murgatroyd in the street.

'Mike!' Her face lit up. 'I never expected to see you in the town in the middle of Tuesday morning.'

'Are you glad?'

A little colour came into her pale pretty face.

'Of course I'm glad,' she said. 'Why shouldn't I be?'

'Why don't you join me for a cup of coffee?' he suggested. 'I was going into Ann's Pantry. At least, I think that's its awful name.'

'All right!' She was wearing a blue silk scarf the colour of her eyes to protect her fair hair from the wind which was blowing along the street. 'I can't stay long, though. I've quite a lot to do at the mill.'

'How's that manager of yours—Eddie Taylor, I think you called him once—getting along?' Mike asked as they walked along the street together.

She frowned. 'Oh, all right, I suppose. I never liked him much when Daddy appointed him, but I have to keep him. I doubt if I could do everything myself.'

'You want to watch him,' Mike said. 'He looks a real villain to me.'

'Oh, Mike, what a thing to say!' she protested as they went into the little coffee shop.

They found a corner table and Mike ordered coffee and biscuits. He took up the subject of Murgatroyd's manager again.

'Couldn't you get someone else instead of Taylor?' he asked. 'I don't like to think of you being at the mercy of a man like that.'

Her eyes twinkled as she smiled at him.

'Oh, Mike, I didn't know you cared!' she chuckled, then in a more serious tone: 'Actually, Eddie Taylor is a very competent man at his job. My father had all the faith in the world in him in the months before he died.'

'That may be so, Ros, but you must remember Taylor had your father to deal with in those days. Sick man though he was, Mr. Murgatroyd would keep a keen eye on his manager. With you it's—well, different.'

'Meaning that because I'm a woman Eddie Taylor's likely to take advantage of me?'

'I suppose that's what I mean!' Seeing the expression on her face he hurried on: 'I'm sorry to put it so crudely, Ros. It's just that—well, I'm fond of you. I don't want to see you exploited by a fly-by-night like Taylor.'

'I'm quite capable of looking after myself, Mike,' she said. 'And now, let's talk about something else. How's your mother?'

'Pretty well, thanks!' He stirred his coffee a little moodily. Why wouldn't Rosalind take his advice and get rid of Taylor? There must be lots of better men to be engaged to do the work.

'I hear Nurse Bailey's leaving,' she said. 'She's been with Earnshaw's a long time. Almost part of the fixtures and fittings!'

He shrugged. 'I've not had much to do with her.'

'Have you anyone else in view?'

'Oh, someone will apply for the job, I suppose, when it's advertised.'

'I don't expect it will be easy to find a suitable person. Most nurses prefer to work with others, not on their own, especially in a business like yours. You may have to do as we do at Murgatroyd's, depend on the trained First Aid personnel amongst our workpeople.'

'You might be right,' he agreed.

'As long as you don't try to lure any of our First Aid people away like those weavers your father persuaded to join Earnshaw's by offering them a pound a week more than they were getting with us!'

'Dad would say that's business!' Mike grinned.

'I'd call it sharp practice,' she said crossly and stood up. 'I must go now, Mike. I haven't time to spend in coffee shops even if you have!'

He watched her trim figure pass out into the street and sighed. She was such a pretty girl, and a sensible and very competent one.

Perhaps that was why he couldn't love her. There seemed little romance about a girl who ran a West Riding textile mill!

When he left the café five minutes later he saw Lucy on the other side of the road. His eyes lit up. Now there was a girl to set a man's pulse racing!

As he crossed the street she turned to look at him. Her dark eyes lit up, her warm lips parted in a welcoming smile.

'Mr. Earnshaw!'

'Hullo, Miss Hirst. Have you had coffee?'

She frowned at the abruptness of the question, then she laughed.

'Why, no!' she admitted.

'Then come and have one with me.'

'But I thought I saw you leaving Ann's Pantry a few seconds ago!'

'I can always drink another cup. Come on!'

He had her elbow in a firm grasp as they crossed to the café. She smiled. What a forceful young man he was. She rather liked him for it.

When they were seated in the café, and the surprised waitress had taken their order, Mike said:

'I've just thought of something. You know Nurse Bailey is leaving Earnshaw's? She's retiring after being with us for centuries.'

'Thirty-two years to be exact!' she smiled.

'I stand corrected! Listen, Lucy, why don't you apply for the job? I'm sure you'd get it.'

'I do hold a rather responsible job in a London teaching hospital, you know, Mr. Earnshaw!'

'Why not call me Mike? It's much shorter and more friendly. I mean to call you Lucy.'

'You're incorrigible!'

'What a long word for so early in the day.' He grinned. 'Well, what about it? Oh, I know your job in London is important, but so is the job at Earnshaw's Mill. They need lots of

36

skilled attention.'

'Why do you think I'd get the job—even if I applied for it? Your father might want an older woman.'

'He wants someone who knows their job, and I'll bet you know yours. Come on, Lucy. Let me take you back to the mill now. In any case, I'd like the Old Man to meet you. Mother was telling him about you and he seemed really interested, especially when he heard you were a nurse.'

So they'd talked about her yesterday, had they? Lucy thought. She found herself wondering what Mr. Earnshaw was really like. Of course she'd seen him once or twice in the streets, mostly at the back of a chauffeur-driven car; and she'd heard her father and brother talk about him, not always in very complimentary terms.

'All right, why not?' she said and Mike, who had expected a refusal, looked at her in surprise.

'You really will come and meet the Old Man?'

'I've said I will.'

'He put some money on the table before the waitress had had time to return with their coffee.

'Come on!' he said, urging her towards the door as if afraid she would change her mind.

He had left his car further along the street. Presently they were driving into the mill yard.

'This way!' Mike said and led Lucy into the office block.

Bessie's mouth fell open as the two young people went into the General Office.

'Hullo, Bessie!' Lucy said.

'Is my father alone?' Mike asked and Bessie nodded.

Mike made for the door at the far side of the big office. Lucy, after winking at Bessie, followed.

Mike, tapping on the door, threw it open. His father looked up with a frown.

'What is it now?' he demanded impatiently.

'I want you to meet someone,' his son said and turned to where Lucy was hesitating on the threshold.

Mr. Earnshaw got to his feet. He looked curiously at Lucy.

'This is Nurse Hirst,' Mike said. 'She's a fully qualified SRN. She might be interested in taking over Nurse Bailey's job.'

Whatever else Matthew Earnshaw was he was a realist. He had tried to persuade Nurse Bailey to stay in her job for another year without success. He had approached several nursing agencies and had not found them at all helpful. Evidently a job in a mill in a place like Lenthwaite was not the sort of thing their nurses would be interested in.

He had already drafted out an advertisement which he meant to send to the

38

nursing journals, but he had little hope that help would come from that source.

He looked at the girl standing before his desk. His wife had told him she had called at the house on the previous day. Mrs. Earnshaw had spoken enthusiastically about this daughter of one of his overlookers, Sam Hirst.

'How do you do, Nurse,' he said. 'I believe your father and brother work for me.'

'Yes! My father's been at Earnshaw's for twenty-eight years. My brother came here from school.'

'And now you want to work here?'

'I didn't say that. I came because your son persuaded me. Actually, I have a job in London.'

'At St. Christopher's. Yes! my wife told me that. To pass their Final examination must mean you are highly qualified. I somehow feel it's a job you'd think twice about giving up.'

'I should have to think things over very carefully.'

'When do you go back to London?'

'In a week's time.'

'Well, there's no hurry. Why not think things over and let me know? Of course I shall have to try other outlets, for I must have someone to take Nurse Bailey's place and pretty soon. However, let me know what you decide and as soon as you can.'

'It might be a good idea if I looked at your

First Aid department. I've not had anything to do with nursing in a mill before.'

Mr. Earnshaw looked at Mike.

'Take her down and introduce her to Nurse Bailey, who can show her round.' He held out his hand. 'Good morning to you, Nurse. I hope I'll hear from you again.'

Lucy felt a little bewildered as she and Mike left his father's office. The interview hadn't gone at all as she had intended it to. She had meant to listen with interest to anything that was suggested, reveal that she was fully tied up at the hospital in London, and promise to think things over in the next few weeks.

Now she had committed herself to a tour of the First Aid department, and had as good as promised to give Mr. Earnshaw a 'Yes' or 'No' in a fairly short time.

'I think my father rather took to you,' Mike said as they left the General Office and made towards the thunder of looms which came from the weaving sheds.

Lucy said nothing to this. His father had taken to her because he knew how difficult it was going to be to fill Nurse Bailey's place. For no other reason.

The First Aid department consisted of three rooms at the end of one of the long weaving sheds. Nurse Bailey was a stout homely person in a white overall and head-dress. She had a kindly face and snow

40

white hair.

When Mike and Lucy appeared she was comforting a young woman who had, apparently, fainted twenty minutes before.

'You're going to be all right, Alice,' she said. 'Just rest there for a little while then go home. You'll be as right as rain in the morning.'

When Mike had introduced Lucy, she took them into her little office.

'The girl's pregnant,' she said. 'She's trying to carry on working as long as she can. I suppose she wants the money.

'I'm sorry to be leaving Earnshaw's in a way,' she said as she showed Lucy round the tiny department. 'It's really worthwhile work here, and there's lots of it. Eight hundred men and women can pose quite a few medical problems in a full working day.'

Apart from the office there was a small rest room and a casualty department.

'Anything I can't handle goes to the hospital, of course,' Nurse Bailey said. 'And of course Dr. Tolson's always available when he's wanted. He comes in three times a week and for emergencies.'

As Mike and Lucy prepared to leave Nurse Bailey smiled.

'I hope you'll take the job, Nurse,' she said. 'I'd like to think another Hirst was coming to work at Earnshaw's. I've known your father for many years, of course. And your brother, too.'

Outside Mike offered to run Lucy home, but she shook her head.

'Shouldn't you be at work yourself?' she asked. 'After all, I've only to walk round the corner.'

He grinned. 'Don't *you* start on me! My father's bad enough.' He looked at her, suddenly serious. 'I hope you'll think about the job, Lucy, in the next week or two. I really do!'

She smiled. 'I promise I'll think about it. But I don't promise to take it.'

Then before he could say any more she turned on her heel and hurried away.


## CHAPTER FOUR

The rest of the holiday passed only too quickly for Lucy. She loved being at home again and as day succeeded day she realised how much her family meant to her.

She helped her mother all she could, and more than once Mrs. Hirst told her how good it was to have her only daughter by her side once more.

Lucy worried about her mother. Often when Mrs. Hirst did not know she was observed, Lucy saw her with her defences down. Then the pain that was her mother's constant companion, showed plainly in the thin face and tensed muscles.

'You should rest more, Mum,' she said over and over again, but Mrs. Hirst only shook her head.

'I don't need to rest, lass,' she replied. 'I'm better moving about. I never was one for taking it easy.'

'But when I've gone back to London there'll be no one to help you.'

'Your dad's very good. And Dick's quite handy when he puts his mind to it.' A smile lit up the thin face. 'I'll be all right, love. Don't worry on my account.'

But Lucy did worry, and she spoke of her anxiety to Bessie when the two girls walked over the moor two days before she was due to go back to London.

'I feel mum needs me,' she said. 'What am I to do, Bessie?'

'There is the job at Earnshaw's,' Bessie said. 'Have you thought any more about it?'

'I can't make up my mind. I wish I could!'

'Well, don't hurry it. You'll have more time to think things over when you're back at the hospital.'

To change the subject Lucy asked:

'Has Dick popped the question yet?' Long ago Bessie had confided to her that she was in love with her brother. Bessie shook her head.

'No, and I don't suppose he ever will. That car of his takes up most of his time and interest just now.'

'He's a fool!' Lucy cried hotly. 'I can't understand him.'

'I shouldn't try,' her friend laughed, then added: 'How's your friendship with Mike Earnshaw progressing?'

It was Lucy's turn to colour.

'He came round again yesterday and asked me to go for a run in his car. I told him I was busy. Actually I was helping Mum to make a dress.'

'That wouldn't please him! A very headstrong young man is our Mr. Michael!'

But Mike did not give up as easily as Lucy hoped he would. The following afternoon he appeared at the door again. He gave her an uneasy smile as if uncertain of his reception.

'I'm going over to Leeds on an errand for my father,' he said. 'I thought you might come along for the ride.'

'I'm not sure—'

'Please do, Lucy! You're going back to London tomorrow. I wanted to spend an hour or so with you before you leave.'

It was a lovely afternoon and Lucy was tempted. Her mother was resting; her father and brother were at the mill, as usual.

'All right,' she said impulsively. 'I'll just get my coat.'

She ran up to tell her mother she would be back by tea-time. Mrs. Hirst smiled.

'He's a persistent young man, that Mike

Earnshaw,' she said. 'How do you feel about him, lass?'

Lucy bent to kiss the pale face.

'Never you mind,' she said. 'So far as I'm concerned he's just a pleasant companion to spend a couple of hours with, nothing more.'

But as she went down the narrow stairs she wondered if perhaps Mike Earnshaw wasn't coming to mean more to her than just an acquaintance. Though she hadn't seen very much of him in the last week she had thought about him a great deal.

They took the road out of Lenthwaite and made for the motorway that would take them almost into the heart of Leeds.

Mike drove fast and Lucy felt the exhilaration of high speed. The wind played with the tendrils of dark hair that had escaped from under the scarf she was wearing.

'Have you thought any more about the job?' he asked.

She knew what he meant. Nurse Bailey's job at Earnshaw's.

'I've not had much time,' she said. 'In any case, I have to go back to London. If I did decide to come back to Lenthwaite I would have to give notice. You can't just walk out of a place like St. Christopher's without some warning. It wouldn't be fair. After all, they trained me for four years. I owe them something in return.'

'I've no doubt you worked hard enough in

those four years,' he said. 'They'd get quite as much out of you as you got out of them.'

She knew he was right but did not say so. Yes! she had worked many many more hours than she need have done. It had been worse when, before nurses' pay was increased, there had been an acute shortage of nursing staff. Lately the situation had eased and if she did decide to leave, she would not feel as guilty as she might have done two years ago.

They went into Leeds and Mike asked Lucy to wait in the car while he went into the big office building to talk to a customer and pick up some samples of cloth.

Lucy, watching him striding back to the car, the parcel under his arm, realised that he attracted her more than she was prepared to admit.

She liked his rugged good looks, the flair with which he wore the expensive leather jacket and tan trousers. He reminded her of someone she had seen on a T.V. commercial advertising some luxury item or other.

He grinned as he slung the parcel into the back seat and sat beside her again.

'It's three o'clock,' he said. 'I'm going to take you somewhere for tea. I think you've earned it.'

'I should be getting back—' she said but the protest was only a formal one.

He drove out of Leeds into the country. Presently he turned up a side road then pulled up outside a half-timbered cottage which had a wooden sign at the gate. On this was painted the single word TEAS.

Though the sun was shining from the clear sky it was still quite chilly. They were early and they were served tea, scones and jam and home-made cakes before a cheerful fire in a big room whose ceiling was supported by an oak beam. There were no other customers.

'It's a bit early for tea,' the proprietress, a stout woman with rosy cheeks and grey hair, said. 'It'll get busy later on.'

It was a happy meal. Lucy, pouring Mike a second cup of tea, felt suddenly sad that at the same time tomorrow she would be two hundred miles away.

As if reading her thoughts Mike said softly: 'When you get back to that hospital of yours do you think you'll miss me?'

She laughed. 'You think a great deal of yourself, don't you?'

'But will you?' he persisted.

'I'll be too busy to miss anybody.'

His hand came across the little table and closed over hers.

'I shall miss you, Lucy,' he said quietly and now all the banter had gone from his voice.

Gently she withdrew her hand.

'You mustn't talk like that, Mike,' she murmured.

'But why not?' he demanded. 'I can't bear the thought of you going away. Promise to

47

come back soon, perhaps to take the job.'

'You know very well I can't promise anything of the kind,' she said. 'All I'll promise is to think things over. If I decide to return to Lenthwaite you'll see me soon enough.'

And with that he had to be content. Soon they were on their way again.

He drove her straight home. Another car was standing outside No. 24. Lucy recognised it as the doctor's.

'Goodbye Lucy!' Mike said. 'I don't suppose you'll have much time for me this evening.'

'I must spend it with my family,' she replied.

He took her hand, then, taking her by surprise, drew her towards him. Just for a moment she lay in his arms; then before she could draw away, he kissed her.

'Lovely Lucy!' he whispered. 'Come back soon!'

Then he let her go. Confused she reached for the door handle, her only thought to get out of the car and into the house.

Suddenly she realised that the door of the house was open. Dr. Tolson was standing on the pavement. Their eyes met.

'Hullo, Miss Hirst,' he said and gave Mike a curious look. 'Your mother seems a little better today, I'm pleased to say.'

'I'm so glad,' Lucy said, keeping her back

turned to Mike. He, as if eager to escape, turned the car and made for the main road.

'You're returning to London tomorrow, I believe,' Dr. Tolson said.

'Yes, by the morning train.'

'I understand you've been offered Nurse Bailey's job at Earnshaw's. I do hope you'll take it. Naturally, for my own part I'd be glad to think I was to work with you at the mill; but I'd also feel happier if you were in Lenthwaite now your mother's not in the best of health.'

Meeting the kindly grey eyes in the good-natured concerned face she found herself wishing he hadn't seen Mike kissing her. He must surely think there was something between Mike and herself, which, of course, there wasn't.

It was on the tip of her tongue to explain this, then she told herself not be be a fool. Dr. Tolson couldn't possibly be interested in her private emotions. In his eyes she was a nurse who could greatly help his patient—her mother—and perhaps do good work at the mill, where he was part-time doctor.

'I've promised to think things over when I get to London,' she said. 'And now, perhaps you'll excuse me, doctor. My mother will be wondering where I've got to.'

She turned and went into the house. He stood there for a few seconds longer staring at the closed door, then with a faint sigh, turned

49

away and went to his car.

★     ★     ★

Lucy arrived back at the hospital on the following afternoon.

'Hullo, Hirst!' her room mate, Rita Aske, greeted, as she walked into the room they shared in the Nurses' Home. 'Had a good time?'

'Marvellous!' Lucy replied. 'What are you doing up here at this time, Rita?'

'They put me on nights just after you left. I got up an hour ago. I just can't sleep during the day. I suppose I'll get used to it about the time I'm due to go on days again!'

As Lucy unpacked her case Rita wanted to know all about her visit to Lenthwaite. Lucy did her best to satisfy her friend's curiosity without giving too much away.

She did, however, mention the offer of the job at Earnshaw's Mill.

'Will you take it?' Rita asked curiously.

'I don't know. I think my mother would like me to but—well, it would be a big step to take. A First Aid department in a Yorkshire mill is very different from being a staff nurse at St. Christopher's.'

'I've a bit of news for you!' Rita's brown eyes twinkled. 'It might help you to make up your mind.'

'What is it?' Lucy asked curiously.

'Your old flame has got the heave-ho!'

Lucy frowned. What did Rita mean unless—

'I don't understand,' she said slowly.

'Mr. Geoffrey Baines, famous surgeon and hospital heart-throb, has had his ring handed back by Miss Ruth Filson. The story's all over the hospital.'

Lucy's heart gave a sudden bound. So Geoffrey was free again! His marriage to Sir Henry's daughter was off.

'I don't know any details,' Rita went on. 'It's just that Sir Henry Filson has had Geoffrey transferred to Mr. Martin's firm. Evidently he finds it a bit embarrassing to have his daughter's ex-boy friend assisting him in the operating theatre.'

'But they'd only been engaged a couple of weeks.'

'One rumour going round is that Ruth Filson was in love with another man who showed little interest in her. She accepted our Geoffrey's proposal with the idea of making this other chap jealous. Apparently she succeeded for the story is that she's going round with the man she really wants after giving Geoffrey the push and that it's only a matter of hours before she announces her engagement to him.'

Lucy was glad when her friend said she had some shopping to do and left her alone.

So Geoffrey was free! She wondered how

long it would be before he got in touch again.

Did she want him to? Did she feel for him in the way she had felt before Ruth Filson had come on the scene? She wasn't sure.

When she had unpacked she went down to the canteen for tea.

As she carried her tray to an unoccupied table a voice which quickened her pulse sounded behind her.

'Lucy! By all that's wonderful! I'd no idea you were back.'

It was Geoffrey, the same tall, slender, good-looking Geoffrey in white coat with his hands thrust deep into the side pockets.

'I'll just get a cup of tea then I'll join you,' he said and turned back to the service hatch.

She sat at the table watching him. He was laughing with the girl who was pouring his cup of tea and she reacted, as all women reacted to his charm, with twinkling eyes and a delighted smile.

Lucy remembered seeing him doing his ward round and how the women patients adored him. He was so good-looking, so amusing, so capable of making a woman feel that she, and only she, was the centre of his universe for that moment of time.

'I suppose it was like that with me,' Lucy thought. 'When I was with him nothing else mattered but that we were together. The whole world became a very wonderful place. When I heard he'd got engaged to Ruth

Filson I thought I'd never know happiness again.'

He had turned away from the serving hatch now and was making towards her table. For a moment his smile had gone, but as he approached it came on again as if a switch had been turned.

'Darling, it's so wonderful to have you back again,' he said, sitting beside her; then with a little frown: 'I suppose you've heard my engagement is off. It's all over the hospital.'

'I did hear something!' Lucy murmured.

'It wouldn't have worked,' he said, stirring his tea. 'I soon found we weren't the same sort of people. Of course, we're still good friends.'

She knew he was lying. He had been jilted—and he didn't like it. Ruth Filson had made him a fool before the whole hospital.

'But now you're back!' he said, his eyes brilliant as they met hers. 'Gosh what an escape I've had. But I don't mind now I've got you back, Lucy.'

She thought: 'Why didn't I see him for what he was before this? How could I ever have let him take me in?'

'Will you see me tonight?' he asked, taking her hand under the table.

She shook her head.

'I'm sorry, Geoffrey, but I shall be busy tonight.'

'But—you won't be going on duty until tomorrow morning.'

She pulled her hand out of his.

'I have a bit of news for you,' she said quietly. 'When I was at home I was offered a job in Lenthwaite. I've decided to take it. I shall be leaving St. Christopher's as soon as they'll let me go.'

'But, Lucy, hang it all, what about me? We were in love! Remember?'

She finished her tea and stood up.

'We *were* in love,' she said slowly. 'Not any more! And now, I've a lot to do. Goodbye, Geoffrey!'

She walked to the door and, without looking back, hurried along the corridor outside.

She had to hand in her resignation then go back to her room and write a letter to her mother saying she would be going back to Lenthwaite as soon as the hospital would release her.

The other letter—to Mr. Earnshaw accepting his offer of a job at the mill—she would write later, perhaps tomrrow.

# PART TWO

# THE MILL

## CHAPTER FIVE

Lucy, hurrying along the platform keeping an eye open for a seat on the crowded train, heard the slam of doors and knew that at any moment the guard would wave his flag.

She must get in somewhere even if she had to stand in the corridor.

'In here, Miss!' a helpful porter called and ushered Lucy and her suitcase into the train, then slammed the door behind her.

A few seconds later the long train drew out of the gloom of King's Cross into the sunshine beyond the platforms.

Lucy made her way along the corridor looking into the compartments as she passed. At last she spotted a seat. A young man slid back the door and lifted her suitcase on to the rack.

As the train got up speed and left London's sprawling suburbs behind, Lucy thought back to that day, four years before, when she had been travelling in the opposite direction. How nervous she had been! A fortnight before she had been up to St. Christopher's for her interview. After a nerve-racking wait a letter had come telling her to take her place as a student nurse in the great teaching hospital.

The time had gone astonishingly quickly. Though the work had been hard, the discipline strict, she had loved being a part of a great institution devoted to curing the sick. Occasionally she had been home-sick but at such times there had usually been an emergency to grapple with, and she had forgotten her own feelings in the pains and discomforts of those she was committed to nursing.

And now she was going home. She smiled to herself remembering the letter she had had from her mother.

'I hope you're doing the right thing, love,' Mrs. Hirst had written. 'I don't want you to feel you're coming home on my account. You've your own life to lead, think on!'

How typical of her mother! Never, never would she admit how much she was enjoying the thought of having her only daughter at home again.

She had had another letter. Mr. Earnshaw had dictated a letter to his secretary appointing her to the position of nurse in charge of the mill's First Aid department.

After Mr. Earnshaw had signed the letter Bessie had scribbled a note at the bottom before slipping it into its envelope.

'Wonderful news! Everybody is thrilled. Looking forward to seeing you. Love. Bessie.'

When the ticket inspector came down the train he looked at Lucy's ticket.

'Change at Leeds for Lenthwaite,' he said.

Lucy, putting the ticket back in her purse, sighed. She had done this journey many times before. There was an hour's wait in Leeds. Oh, well, she'd have to have a cup of tea in the refreshment room and possess herself in patience. It wouldn't be the first time she'd done that!

When a passenger left the train at Peterborough she moved into the vacant corner seat. She closed her eyes and, because she had had a restless night, she went to sleep almost immediately. She did not wake until the express was a few miles from Leeds.

Rain was falling from a leaden sky. How often she had left London in sunshine and returned to weeping skies in Yorkshire!

She left the train and made her way towards the barrier. As she showed her ticket a voice behind her exclaimed:

'Miss Hirst!'

She looked round in surprise. Dr. Tolson was smiling at her as he followed her through the barrier. She returned his smile.

'Are you going on to Lenthwaite?' he asked.

'Yes, there's an hour to wait for the connection.'

'No need for that,' he said briskly. 'I've been to London for the day. My car's in the car park. I'll give you a lift home.'

'Thank you,' she said, a little confused. She hoped he wasn't just offering her a lift out of politeness.

But already he had taken her suitcase and was turning towards the car park.

'Your mother said you were coming home today,' he said. 'I'd have looked out for you on the train but, of course, I didn't know what time of day you would be travelling.'

'Do you often go up to London for the day?' she asked because she felt she had to make conversation.

'Not often! I had to attend a meeting at lunch time. A doctor's organisation I belong to. I represent the local committee which includes doctors in Lenthwaite and round about. I just managed to get the afternoon train, otherwise I would have had to spend the night in a London hotel.'

He put her suitcase on the back seat of his car and half a minute later they were driving out of the station into the rainy evening.

She stole a glance at him as they took the Lenthwaite road. In profile he had a short straight nose and a firm chin. His eyes were narrowed as he peered ahead as the rain beat on the windscreen. There was something almost forbidding about his appearance, but this impression was dispelled as, probably becoming aware of her scrutiny, he turned to smile at her. It was a rather shy smile which lit up his grey eyes and softened the contours of his lean face.

'Mr. Earnshaw told me that he had appointed you in Nurse Bailey's place,' he said. 'May I say how glad I am that you'll be in charge of the First Aid department at the mill?'

'Thank you,' she murmured.

'I'm glad you're coming back to Lenthwaite for another reason,' he went on, his eyes on the wet road again. 'Ever since she knew you had taken the job your mother's condition has improved dramatically. I saw her yesterday and she looked better than I've seen her look for some months.'

'I'm so glad,' she said.

What a nice man he was! He must have hundreds of patients in Lenthwaite and the surrounding countryside yet he could go out of his way to take such an interest in her mother.

Impulsively she said: 'My mother—and father—must be most grateful to you for looking after her so well, doctor.'

'I do the best I can for all my patients,' he said a trifle uncomfortably as if he did not like praise.

He was silent for several minutes after that.

Lucy, watching the wipers clearing the rain from the windscreen, began to feel almost mesmerised. She blinked her eyes. She must keep awake. What would Dr. Tolson think if she dropped off?

In desperation she asked:

'How do you like Lenthwaite, Dr. Tolson? I believe you took Dr. Bancroft's practice over about a year ago.'

He nodded. 'I like it very well. It is very different from the Midlands where I was assistant in a practice in Birmingham.'

'My mother says you have a little girl. How old is she?'

'Six!' There was a soft note in his voice now. 'She goes to the local school.'

After a short pause he said:

'It wasn't easy at first. Margy missed her little friends at the school she attended before we came to Lenthwaite. Then there were her mother's friends. They made a great fuss of her when my wife died. She was very lonely at first when we came to Lenthwaite; but I think she's adapted very well in the last six months.'

What a tragedy it was to lose one's wife so early in life, what a problem for a man left to bring up a young child amongst strangers, Lucy thought.

But Dr. Tolson seemed to have coped very well.

'I was lucky in finding Mrs. Barrett,' he

said. 'She's the widow of one of the workmen at Earnshaw's mill. Mr. Barrett died suddenly two years ago. She looks after the house and Margy. Fortunately the child took to her right away.'

'Do you live in Dr. Bancroft's old house?' Lucy asked.

He nodded. 'Yes, I took it over. It seemed the simplest thing to do. It's a bit old-fashioned for my taste and I dread to think what Sylvia would have thought about it. But—well, it serves its purpose, and of course all the surgery facilities are there.'

Lucy wondered what Sylvia had looked like. Was she pretty or plain, managing or retiring, smart or dowdy? From the brief mention Dr. Tolson had made of his wife she formed a picture of a friendly well-dressed woman with decided ideas on clothes and the furnishings that should go in a modern home.

'Are you looking forward to your work at Earnshaw's?' the doctor asked.

'Very much! It will be very different from what I've been used to but—well, I suppose in a way it will be a challenge.'

'There's much more to it than meets the eye,' he said reflectively. 'When I took the job on I thought there'd be little to do. But I find I can hardly get through the work in the three days I spend at the mill.'

The rain had stopped as they drove into Lenthwaite. They passed an old Victorian

61

villa on the outskirts of the little town. Lucy's eyes went to the gate which let on to the short drive.

Several times she had gone up to the old house with her mother when she was suffering from some childish complaint.

There were two brass plates on the gatepost now: a very old one with the name almost polished away, and a new one bearing the name of the newcomer.

Dr. Tolson had seen Lucy's glance. He laughed.

'I hope you're admiring my new plate! It's my first. I hope it will be there as long as Dr. Bancroft's.'

'But he was in practice here for nearly forty years!' she exclaimed, then coloured wondering if he would think her impertinent in suggesting that he might want to go away from Lenthwaite when he tired of the little place.

But he only smiled. 'That's what I mean,' he said quietly. 'If I can do as good a job as Dr. Bancroft I'll be quite satisfied. I'm not a very ambitious man.'

They drove through the town and Lucy was surprised how many people waved recognising the doctor's car. Dr. Tolson might only have been in Lenthwaite just over a year but he was already accepted by the people of the little town.

'I'll come in and see your mother now I'm

here,' he said drawing up at Lucy's home. 'I think she might need another prescription for her tablets.'

Lucy opened the house door and he followed her along the passage to the kitchen.

But it was empty. Hearing footsteps upstairs Lucy made for the staircase.

'Mother! Dad! I'm home,' she cried.

Her father came to look down at her. His face was worried.

'Your mother's in bed,' he called. 'She said she didn't feel very well when I got home from the mill so I persuaded her to go to bed. She didn't want to, I can tell you!'

'I'd better look at her,' Alan Tolson said to Lucy. 'You go first and I'll follow in a couple of minutes.'

Lucy hurried upstairs. She found Mrs. Hirst lying, white and frail-looking, in the big double bed. She held out her hand as Lucy went into the room.

'Lucy love, you're early!' she said. 'We didn't expect you for another hour. In fact, Dick said he'd meet your train when it reached Lenthwaite.'

'Dr. Tolson was on the same train,' Lucy said, kissing her pale cheek. 'He's brought me home so he can take a look at you while he's here.'

'He needn't bother,' Mrs. Hirst said. 'There's nowt wrong with me that a good night's sleep won't cure.'

But there came a knock at the door and the young doctor came into the room.

'Now, Mrs. Hirst, what's all this?' he cried cheerfully.

'Why everyone gets upset because a body can feel a bit tired I'll never know!' his patient grumbled.

Lucy went out of the room with her father. She kissed him fondly as they stood on the landing outside the bedroom door.

'How are you, Dad?' she asked.

'I'm fine,' he said, then glancing at the closed door: 'She looked quite ill when I got in for my tea. Of course, being your mother, she had to give me my food before she'd give in. But when I saw how she was I got her up to bed.'

'It was the best thing,' Lucy said.

They waited for the doctor. Presently he came out on to the landing.

'You can go in to her now,' he said. 'It's nothing to worry about, though she should stay in bed for a day or two. Here's a prescription. Send Dick for it. Mr. Hailey the chemist will have it made up if he goes round to the side entrance.'

'Very well, doctor,' Mr. Hirst said, taking the folded piece of paper.

Lucy said:

'Thank you for the lift from Leeds, doctor. It was very kind of you.'

'I ought to thank you,' he smiled. 'I hate

driving by myself, especially in rain.'

He said a cheerful goodnight and disappeared down the narrow stairs. Lucy heard him speaking to her brother who had just come into the house.

She turned and made into the bedroom again. Her mother's face lit up as she appeared.

'Fancy Dr. Tolson giving you a lift from Leeds,' she marvelled. 'He's a really nice young man,' and added darkly: 'Better than some we read about in the papers these days.'

'He told me a little about his wife and child,' Lucy said. 'He seems to be coping fairly well with the help of a woman called Mrs. Barrett.'

'She's old Arthur Barrett's widow,' Mrs. Hirst declared. 'She's over sixty but still fairly active. She'll do very well for him. I don't doubt. That is, until he marries again.'

'You think he might?' Lucy exclaimed.

'It'd be a pity if he didn't,' her mother said. 'A good-looking young man like that with a motherless child to care for. Of course, he'll get married, and the sooner the better, I should hope!'

'I don't suppose there are many women he'd want to marry in Lenthwaite. The ones I know aren't likely to be much in his line.'

'He'll find someone, never you fear,' Mrs. Hirst said and gave Lucy a look which brought the colour into her cheeks.

Changing the subject abruptly Lucy said: 'You're to stay in bed for a few days. Oh, I know what you're going to say. That we can't get along without you. Well, we'll have to try, won't we? I'm quite capable of looking after one semi-invalid after caring for a ward full of cantankerous old men, which I've been doing for the last six months.'

'I'm right enough,' her mother protested, but Lucy, tucked her in, bent and kissed her faded cheek.

'You'll do as you're told,' she said quietly and her mother grinned seeing the twinkle in her eyes.

'Very well, Nurse,' she said with a chuckle; then taking Lucy's hand: 'Oh, lass, you've no idea what a relief it is to have you back home. I've missed you so very much.'

'Try to sleep now,' Lucy said and then, as she turned to the door, she was surprised to find that there were tears in her eyes.

## CHAPTER SIX

The following Monday morning Lucy reported at the mill. Her mother had benefited from a couple of days in bed and was now in full charge of her kitchen again.

'It's no use trying to change her, Lucy love,' Mr. Hirst said, after Lucy had

66

protested when her mother insisted on helping with the washing up when she'd only been downstairs for an hour.

Bessie was at her desk when Lucy entered the General Office.

'Mr. Earnshaw's had to go to Bradford on business,' Bessie said. 'He left a note on my desk to tell you to take over the First Aid Department.'

'But isn't Nurse Bailey still here?' Lucy asked.

'No, she left last Friday evening. Evidently her sister in Bristol has been taken ill and she had to go to her. I think she'd intended staying on here a day or two to see you settled in the new job. I'm sorry, Lucy.'

'It's all right. It's often best to be thrown in at the deep end; then you're forced to swim.'

She made her way towards the thunder of the looms in the weaving sheds. Bessie had given her the key of her new quarters and soon she was making herself fully conversant with the drugs in the cupboard in the office and the equipment in the small casualty room.

She was wearing a print dress and apron. As she adjusted her white head-dress, which apparently Mr. Earnshaw liked his First Aid nurse to wear whilst on duty, her first patient arrived.

This was a stout middle-aged woman whose right eye was almost closed.

'Hullo, what's the trouble?' Lucy asked, and after she had discovered that the woman's name was Mrs. Bodger, and that a boil on her eyelid was causing her a great deal of pain, she said: 'You'd better go and see your doctor. That boil needs medical attention.'

'But can't you do something, Miss? I don't want to sit in no doctor's waiting room.'

'I'm afraid it's a job for the doctor. Who is your doctor, by the way?'

'Dr. Tolson.'

'I'll ring him and say you're coming. His surgery hours are from nine o'clock until ten.'

'All right, if you say so,' Mrs. Bodger grumbled and took herself off.

Lucy rang Alan Tolson's number which, with other information, had been typed and pinned to a small notice board on the wall.

He answered almost immediately.

'It's Nurse Hirst,' Lucy said. 'I'm sending a Mrs. Bodger to you. She's got a nasty boil on her eye. She says she's a patient of yours.'

'I'll do my best for her,' he promised, then added: 'How are you enjoying your first day on duty?'

'I've hardly had time to tell. I didn't get here until nine o'clock and it's barely half-past yet.'

He laughed. 'I might pop in and see how you're getting on later in the day,' he said and then rang off.

She felt relieved at the prospect of Alan

Tolson's coming visit. Though she knew she was fully competent to handle anything that might arise in the next few hours, it was nice to think that she would have a little friendly support on her first day at the mill.

How different it was sitting here in the small office with the dull thunder of the looms all about her when she had always been used to the bustle and rush of a ward in a busy hospital.

In the next two hours her only visitors were two rather sheepish sixteen year olds. One had an ugly gash on his hand. The other addressed Lucy.

'My mate's cut 'is 'and, Miss,' he said.

'Come in here,' Lucy said and led the way into the little Casualty Room.

'How did this happen?' she asked.

It was a muddled story but in the end she got at the truth. It was one of their jobs to move heavy skeps from one end of the weaving shed to the other. They had 'been larking about', as the uninjured lad put it, and his friend had fallen and cut his hand on a piece of metal projecting from the skep.

Lucy attended to the wound, then as she was bandaging it, the door opened and a voice said:

'So here you are! Hard at work, I see.'

She looked round and saw Mike Earnshaw's smiling face. The two boys exchanged scared glances. Would she give

69

them away, they both wondered.

'Speak to the overlooker and ask him to give you a lighter job for the rest of the day,' she said to her patient. 'And keep the wound covered up until it heals. In fact, you'd better let me have another look at it tomorrow morning. I may want to change the dressing.'

'Thanks, Nurse,' the boy said, then with his friend close behind he slid past Mike and disappeared.

'What was all that about?' Mike asked.

'He cut his hand and very sensibly came to me with it,' Lucy said, tidying up.

He lost interest in the two boys.

'It's wonderful to find that you've actually started on the job, Lucy,' he said. 'I've been keeping my fingers crossed in case you changed your mind.'

'Why should I?'

He shrugged. 'It does happen sometimes. After all, it must have been a big wrench to tear yourself away from an interesting life in a big hospital and come to a small place like Lenthwaite to a job where you'll be by yourself most of the time.'

'There were other considerations that made up my mind for me,' she murmured.

'Your mother? How is she, by the way? Your father told me she hasn't been too well again.'

She wondered what he would say if she told him that one most important reason why she

70

had come back to Lenthwaite: that she had found Geoffrey Baines out to be a liar, a man without any principles where love was concerned. When he had been jilted by the girl he had hoped would further his career he had expected to find his old girl friend waiting, eager to have him back.

But perhaps Mike would not be interested to hear about Geoffrey. All he seemed concerned about was that she was in Lenthwaite and likely to stay there.

'My mother's better than she was,' she said in reply to his question. 'Of course, she ought to rest more, and I'm hoping I'll be able to see she does now I'm living at home.'

'How about coming out to dinner with me this evening?' he suggested. 'There's a nice little restaurant just opened on the moor road. It's supposed to be quite good.'

She shook her head with a smile.

'It's very good of you to ask me,' she said, 'but most of my time will be taken up at home in the evenings, at least until my mother's a little stronger.'

He frowned but did not press her. As a knock sounded on the door he turned to go.

'Another patient,' he said, but as the door opened he saw Dr. Tolson on the threshold.

'Hullo, Doc!' he said. 'I suppose, like me, you've called to see how Nurse Hirst is settling in.'

'Something like that,' the young doctor

71

smiled.

'Then I'll be getting back to my office.' He glanced back at Lucy. 'I hope it won't be long before we can have dinner together. Cheerio!'

Then he was gone. Alan Tolson looked a little uncertainly at Lucy.

'I'm sorry I interrupted you,' he said. 'I didn't know Mr. Earnshaw was with you.'

She remembered suddenly how he had seen her with Mike once before: outside her home when Mike had taken her in his arms and kissed her. It was on the tip of her tongue to tell him there was nothing between her and Mike, but she didn't speak. After all, why should she assume that he was at all interested in either Mike or herself, or in any feeling there might be between them?

'I saw Mrs. Bodger,' he said coming further into the room. 'You were quite right to send her to me with that boil. It was giving her a great deal of pain. Have you had anyone else in for treatment?'

'Just a boy with a cut hand.'

'I shall be in tomorrow morning to check up on several workpeople who have returned to the mill after illness. I've also several youngsters to examine before they start on their new jobs. Perhaps you'll give me a hand.'

'Of course! What time will you come in?'

'After my morning surgery, about half past ten. We should be able to get through by late

72

afternoon allowing an hour for lunch.'

She thought he looked tired. She wondered if he had been called out in the night. He checked a yawn and as if he had guessed what she was thinking, smiled.

'A patient decided to have her baby a week early,' he said. 'I didn't get to bed till four o'clock this morning.'

'I'll make some coffee,' she said, but he shook his head.

'Thanks, but I must get on. I've a long list of visits.' He made for the door. 'I'll see you in the morning.'

Then he was gone and she went back to her little office to look through a file of notes Nurse Bailey had left her.

'Sarah Ollerenshaw (56) a diabetic. Watch her. She sometimes forgets her insulin.'

'William Riley (44). Bad hay fever in summer. Tell him to stay at home till the attack is over.'

'Hannah Rawson (28). Has had bad attacks of asthma from time to time.'

And so it went on, a painstaking, loving investigation of the hundreds of workpeople who had been in Nurse Bailey's charge for years.

'No wonder everybody loved her,' Lucy thought, closing the file. 'They must have been like children to her.'

She wondered if she would come to look upon the mill workers as her predecessor had:

as a big family whose health was her main concern, her whole life.

'I suppose it depends on how long I keep the job,' she thought. 'Maybe if I stay here over thirty years, like Nurse Bailey, I might get as devoted to my patients as she did.'

She found the thought rather depressing. Thirty years! Why, she would be in her fifties, then!

Later she closed and locked the outer door and went home for lunch.

'How did you enjoy your first morning, then?' her mother asked, bringing a steak and kidney pie to the table.

'I didn't have much to do,' Lucy replied, making her mother sit down while she cut portions of the pie for her father and brother.

She helped her mother and herself then sat down. Her father smiled.

'I think you had young Bottomley in with a cut hand?' And when Lucy nodded. 'Him and his pal, Alf Holden, are always fooling about. They'll be getting the push if they don't watch out. I've got my eyes on them!'

That afternoon Lucy went over the equipment in the First Aid department. She soon found that little appeared to have been replaced for a very long time. Evidently Nurse Bailey had been content to work with mostly out of date instruments which, in Lucy's view, were more fitted to a medical museum. The drugs cupboard, too, contained

74

few modern drugs. She made a note to talk this aspect of her work over with Alan Tolson when he came to the mill in the morning.

Her only patient that afternoon was a weaver who said she had given her knee a painful knock on one of the looms. Lucy had just made a pot of tea in the little office and, after she had examined the knee and suggested a sit-down for half an hour, she offered the woman a cup.

'That's good of you, Nurse,' the other said and settled herself comfortably in one of the office chairs.

Mrs. Robson was about thirty-five years old. She was stout and a little short of breath. She stirred three spoonfuls of sugar into her tea and asked Lucy how she was enjoying her first day at Earnshaw's Mill.

'Very much!' Lucy said and secretly made a resolve to look Mrs. Robson up in Nurse Bailey's file of notes. She believed she might find her listed there.

'We all miss Nurse Bailey very much,' Mrs. Robson sighed. 'Always good for a talk and a bit of advice.'

'I hope you'll look upon me in the same way,' Lucy said and wondered how many others who worked for Mr. Earnshaw saw a visit to the nurse as an excuse for a sit-down and a chat. Mrs. Robson had even timed her arrival when she was almost certain to be offered a cup of tea!

'How does your knee feel now?' Lucy asked after she had removed her visitor's cup.

Mrs. Robson, who was in the middle of a complaint about her eighty-year-old mother, who lived with her, broke off in mid-sentence.

'My knee?' she frowned, then recovering: 'Oh, much better, I think.'

She stood up and took a tentative step or two.

'It seems normal again,' Lucy said drily. 'I think you'd better go back to work.'

'Perhaps a few more minutes—'

'No, now!' There was a twinkle in her eyes. 'Admit it, now, Mrs. Robson. There really isn't anything wrong with your knee, now is there?'

The other avoided her glance then suddenly laughed.

'Not much,' she admitted. 'But it was worth a try. I get so fed up standing at that loom all day.'

When she had gone Lucy opened Nurse Bailey's file. She soon found Mrs. Robson's name.

'A real lead swinger. When she wants to work she's as good as anyone in the mill. Look out for her about tea-time with some cock and bull story. You'll get used to her!'

Lucy, looking up at five o'clock after the mill buzzer had sounded, sighed.

If this was a typical day she was going to

76

find herself missing the rush and bustle of St. Christopher's where she had hardly ever finished one job before another had presented itself.

Suddenly she thought:

'But tomorrow will be different when Dr. Tolson comes.'

And she was surprised at herself, as she walked the short distance home, for so looking forward to spending the next day in the company of a young doctor who had chosen to make his life in a rather drab little mill town when the whole wide world was before him.

## CHAPTER SEVEN

Alan Tolson gave a sigh of relief as he heard the outer door close behind his last patient. Surgery had been busier than usual that morning and he was already late for his day at the mill.

Mercifully he had only two visits to make and he could fit those in later in the day. Neither was urgent.

He crossed to the waiting room and locked the outer door, then he went back into the consulting room again, picked up his bag and made for the main part of the house.

His housekeeper was crossing the hall.

'Oh, Mrs. Barrett, I shan't be in for a meal at mid-day, you know,' he said. 'It's my day at the mill. You'll see that Margy has something, won't you?'

'I'll see to her, Doctor, never fear,' she smiled.

She was a big boned woman with a placid face under thinning white hair. She wore a flowered overall and was carrying a duster.

'I'm just going to give the sitting room a going over,' she declared. 'I suppose you'll be at the mill until about four o'clock. I'll telephone you there if you're wanted.'

'Very well!' He made for the front door. 'Stay with Margy till I get back.'

'You can rely on me, Doctor! Goodbye!'

He went out to his car which was waiting in front of the house. As he started the engine he thought: 'I'm lucky to have someone like Mrs. Barrett! She's kind and honest—and Margy likes her.'

As he drove through Lenthwaite to the mill he thought sadly of his dead wife. How different everything had been since Sylvia had died! The shock of her sudden death was passing now, but it had left him with a feeling of awful emptiness, a loneliness which was just as acute when he was with other people as in the long sleepless hours at night.

And though Margy was a bright cheerful child, he was sure she missed her mother more than she would admit. More than once

78

he had heard her crying as she lay in bed, and though he had gone to her, he had known that in spite of his loving words he had failed to comfort her.

He reached the mill to find the passage outside the First Aid department filled with a chattering queue of women waiting for his arrival.

Lucy had a cup of coffee waiting for him.

'I wasn't quite sure of the procedure,' she said. 'I gather that you see them in groups of a dozen at a time. At least, that's what one of the women told me.'

'There certainly seem more than a dozen waiting outside at this moment,' he said.

'Had I better send some back to work until you're ready for them?'

'I think so! Mr. Earnshaw won't like it if he comes along and sees that mob wasting time gossiping out there.'

Lucy went out into the corridor. The weavers, who had been chattering and laughing together, enjoying this break in the monotonous routine of their day, fell silent.

'The doctor will see the ones who've come back after being ill first,' she said. 'You others must go back to your looms for half an hour. At a quarter past eleven you can return, and the doctor will see you then.'

Grumbling, they moved away. Lucy went back into her office. Alan Tolson smiled.

'I'll see them in the next room,' he said.

'Tell the first one to come in.'

'You'll find their cards on the table,' she told him. 'I got them all out earlier.'

'Good girl!'

He made for the door. After giving him a minute's grace she went to call the first woman in.

She had just returned from a convalescent home after an operation for gall stones. She was a thin anxious little woman called Gibbs. Obviously she was keen to get back to her loom after such a long lay-off.

'And how do you feel, Mrs. Gibbs?' Dr. Tolson asked, telling her to take a seat in front of the table at which he was sitting.

'Ready to start work, Doctor,' she said. 'I feel fine.'

'Hmm!' He took her temperature, then her blood pressure.

'You ought to take it easy for another week, Mrs. Gibbs,' he said.

'Nay, Doctor, I'm right enough!' she exclaimed. 'I need the money. This sick pay isn't enough for me and two childer.'

'But your husband?—'

She scowled. 'My husband left me three years ago, Doctor. I haven't seen sight or sound of him since 1973.'

He frowned then made a decision.

'I'll tell you what, Mrs. Gibbs,' he said. 'Come back half-time for a week, then, if I pass you as fit, you can go back to full time.'

It was the best he could do for her and she had to accept it.

The next woman had been away for a month after being knocked down by a car as she was leaving work. Alan glanced at her card.

'How's the leg, Mrs. Topham?' he asked.

'Still gives me a bit of pain, Doctor. But I can manage quite well with a stick.'

'Well enough to start work again?'

'I don't see why not!' She was a woman in her early fifties with a jolly red face and dyed black hair. 'My husband says if I can stand up to cook a meal I can stand up at my loom.'

'You're going to the hospital for physiotherapy for the leg?'

'Yes! It seems a little better every time I go.'

'Well, you can start work, I suppose, but if you have any more trouble you must come back and see me again.'

'Very well, Doctor!' She hobbled out and another woman took her place.

And so it went on until those who had returned after being off ill or injured had been disposed of.

'Now for the young ladies!' Alan grinned.

'But there weren't any men,' Lucy frowned.

'I see them last of all, late this afternoon. It's Ladies First in the Earnshaw establishment.'

The first of the girls were soon disposed of. These were new employees, some of whom had left school at the end of the last term.

It was the law that they must be seen by the doctor before taking up their work permanently.

Most of them giggled and flashed their eyes at the young doctor. And he laughed and talked with them putting them immediately at their ease.

Only one girl failed to come up to the doctor's rigorous examination, a pale-faced girl with light blue eyes and very fair hair. She stifled a cough as Alan examined her.

'How long have you had that cough, Alice?' he asked.

'Oh, since last summer. I got wet one day when we went off, my mam and dad and me, to the sea. I caught a chill, I reckon. The cough's hung around all winter.'

He listened carefully to her chest then hooked his stethoscope around his neck again. Just for a moment his eyes met Lucy's. She knew what he was thinking.

Alice Smith was not fit to work in a weaving shed.

'Alice, I'm going to give you a note for the hospital,' he said looking at the girl with his kindly smile. 'I'd like them to make a few tests. It's purely a precautionary measure, nothing to be frightened about. And I'll also drop a line to your usual doctor. That's Dr.

Edmunds, I believe?'

'But—the job?'

'I'd rather you didn't start just yet. Later, maybe.'

She started to cry. Weak helpless tears, ran down her pale cheeks.

'I don't know what my dad will say!' she sobbed.

'Surely he won't mind us getting you fit and strong before you start work, Alice,' he said gently. 'I'll tell you what. I've got your address. I'll pop in and have a word with your parents this evening. How's that?'

She thanked him tremulously and departed clutching the note for the hospital.

'Poor kid!' Alan said. 'She was so looking forward to taking her first wage packet home.'

She thought: 'What a nice man he is. How many doctors would have added extra work to a busy day just to reassure someone he'd never seen before in his life.'

The phone in Lucy's office rang. She went to answer it.

Bessie's voice sounded in the receiver:

'Mr. Earnshaw wants you and Dr. Tolson to have lunch in the directors' dining room at half-past twelve, Lucy.'

'Are you sure he wants me—as well as the doctor?' Lucy gasped.

'He most certainly does,' Bessie chuckled. 'He made quite a point of saying so. I think he wants to ask how you're getting on.'

Lucy went back to Dr. Tolson.

'Mr. Earnshaw wants us to have lunch with him in the directors' dining room,' she said. 'At half-past twelve.'

He frowned. 'And I was hoping to snatch a sandwich and beer in a local pub.'

'I'd better send a message home with my father saying I'll not be in until this evening.'

'I'll hold the fort while you look for him,' he offered.

'Thanks!'

She turned and made her way out of the First Aid department. Going down the passage she pushed open a heavy wooden door. The noise of a hundred looms deafened her as she went into the long building. The air was heavy with the oily smell of wool. The morning sunlight slanted in through the glass roof. The weavers looked at her curiously as she passed. One called something to a friend at a neighbouring loom. The other laughed and called back. No sound reached Lucy's ears. These women, working for years in the racket of a weaving shed, had long ago learnt to lip-read.

She found her father at the end of the long building.

'I shan't be home at dinner time,' she shouted. 'Let mum know then she won't wait.'

'All right, love,' he shouted back. 'Don't

84

tell me Dr. Tolson's taking you out!'

She shook her head. 'No, Mr. Earnshaw!' she replied, then as his mouth opened in amazement, she gave him a mischievous wink and hurried away.

The director's dining room was in the mill's administrative block. It was a small panelled room, with, in the centre, a highly polished mahogany table. This was set for lunch with five places. A photograph of the Earnshaw Mill had been framed and held pride of place on one of the walls.

Mr. Earnshaw and a tall grey-haired man were standing at a small table set with bottles which stood against the wall.

'Ah, Doctor! And you, Nurse!' Mr. Earnshaw cried as Alan and Lucy appeared. 'Come over here and have a glass of sherry before we eat.'

As they approached Mr. Earnshaw indicated his companion.

'I don't think you've met Mr. Hartley, the company secretary, have you, Nurse?' And when Lucy shook her head: 'Nurse Hirst joined us yesterday, Bob. Her father and brother work for the firm. In fact, Sam Hirst's been with us nearly as long as Nurse Bailey.'

Lucy felt her hand taken and met a pair of kindly brown eyes.

'How are you settling down, Nurse?' Mr. Hartley asked, after he had nodded at Alan

Tolson, whom he obviously knew.

'Very well, I think,' Lucy replied, 'though of course I've only been here a very short time.'

'What would you like to drink, Nurse?' Mr. Earnshaw asked. 'Sweet sherry or dry?'

'I'd rather have tomato juice, please,' she replied. She had seen some bottles at the back of the table.

He laughed. 'Ah, well, I suppose someone has to drink the stuff!'

He handed glasses round then frowned as the door opened and his son came into the room.

'So there you are!' he said sharply. 'I'm doing your job for you.'

'Sorry, Dad!' Mike said. 'Got caught up with a phone call just as I was leaving the office. I'll pour the next round.'

Mike gave himself a drink and raised his glass to Lucy.

'Hoping you stay with us a very long time, Nurse,' he said and something in his eyes set her pulse racing.

She wondered what his father would think if he saw Mike looking at her like that. Fortunately Mr. Earnshaw had turned to discuss something with Mr. Hartley so did not notice.

After a little desultory conversation the small party was called to the table by a woman in an overall who proceeded to serve lunch. There was soup, roast beef and Yorkshire pudding and a meringue flan. Coffee followed.

Mr. Earnshaw sat at the top of the table with Lucy and Alan on his left, and the company secretary and Mike on his right. The talk was of business. Mr. Earnshaw mentioned that a big order had come from the Middle East only that morning.

By the time the sweet course arrived this subject and its off-shoots had been exhausted. Mr. Earnshaw, spurning the sweet, lit a cigar and looked at Alan Tolson.

'And how are the new girls, Doctor?' he asked.

'You mean the ones I examined this morning?'

'Yes, of course. All fit and well, I hope. Getting the right kind of lass isn't easy these days. They all want too much money. Prefer to work in shops and hairdressing saloons.'

'They all seemed a very good lot,' Alan replied. 'Unfortunately I had to send one girl for some tests to hospital.'

'Tests! Tests! What sort of tests!' Mr. Earnshaw exclaimed. He was scowling now.

'I'd rather not say any more,' the young doctor said.

'Who was she? What was her name?'

Alan frowned. He was obviously reluctant to discuss Alice Smith's case publicly like this.

'Her name's Alice Smith,' he said. 'I believe her father works in the stores.'

'Joe Smith's lass, eh? What do you imagine is wrong with her, doctor, that makes you feel you couldn't pass her?'

Alan shook his head.

'Doctors don't discuss their patients, Mr. Earnshaw, as you well know,' he smiled.

The other seemed about to argue, then, looking into the young man's determined face, he gave a short laugh and looked at his son.

'Go and see where that woman's got to with the coffee,' he snapped, and turned to the company secretary with some remark about a customer he was going to visit in Manchester on the following day.

The lunch party broke up ten minutes later. Mr. Earnshaw nodded curtly at Lucy as she thanked him for the meal.

'Come to me if at any time you have any worries,' he said. 'I'm glad you see you're fitting into things so well.'

Then he turned back to the company secretary.

'Come to my office, Bob,' he said, taking the other's arm. 'There are one or two things I want to discuss with you before the balance sheet goes to the auditors.'

When the two older men had gone from the room Mike chuckled as he looked at the mill doctor.

'You certainly didn't come out of that any too well, old man,' he said. 'My revered parent expects to know every little thing about the people who work for him, even to the state of their health.'

Alan coloured. 'He ought to know very well that I'm not at liberty to discuss such matters publicly. The girl's health is a matter between her and her doctor.'

'You know that, I know that, Nurse Hirst knows that but, unfortunately, my dear father doesn't. Ah, well, take comfort from the fact that he'll have forgotten all about Alice Smith in ten minutes from now. Much more important matters will have claimed his attention.'

Alan looked at Lucy.

'We'd better be getting back,' he said. 'We've a lot to get through this afternoon.'

As they made for the door Mike called after Lucy:

'Will you wait a moment, Lucy? There's something I want to ask you.'

Alan glanced at her. 'I'll go ahead,' he said, and, opening the door, disappeared.

She frowned as she turned back to the other young man.

'What is it, Mr. Earnshaw?' she asked.

She disliked the way he had detained her. It must seem to Alan Tolson that a special relationship existed between them. She remembered how Alan had seen Mike kiss

89

her outside her father's house.

'There's a good film on at a cinema in Bradford,' he said. 'I thought we might see it tonight.'

She shook her head. 'I'm afraid not! There's a great deal to do when I get home in the evening.'

He tried to take her hand.

'But, Lucy, all work and no play—you know the old saying? Surely your mother could spare you for one evening.'

She drew her hand away from his.

'Thank you but it's not possible,' she said, and, turning, made for the door.

She felt very angry as she made her way back to her own department. She wondered if Mike had called her back to make Dr. Tolson think there was more between them than was actually the case.

Yet why should he? To take her out to the cinema was nothing out of the ordinary. Perhaps she was being just a little childish.

She liked Mike. She had to admit that to herself. Perhaps she liked him more than she was prepared to concede.

When she pushed open the door of her new domain she had begun to tell herself that she had been foolish and unkind to slap Mike down so ruthlessly.

Perhaps he would not ask her to go out with him again. Well, if that happened it would be her own fault.

She found Dr. Tolson waiting in her office. He looked at his watch.

'Almost two o'clock,' he said. 'The first of the afternoon people should be along at any moment.'

As if his words were a signal there came a knock at the outer door. Lucy went to admit a nervous sixteen-year-old who gave her a shy smile and said her name was Marilyn Cooper.

'In here,' Lucy said. 'The doctor will see you at once.' She added in a low voice: 'There's nothing to be afraid of, Marilyn. It's just a routine examination to make sure you're quite fit to work in the mill. All school leavers have to go through it.'


## CHAPTER EIGHT

'I don't like it, Dick, and that's a fact!'

Sam Hirst looked across the table at his son.

'But, Dad, there's never been a strike at Earnshaw's in over forty years!' Dick cried. 'Oh, I know there have been a lot of grumbles about pay in the last few months, but as Mr. Earnshaw's never allowed his workfolk to belong to a union, who would be likely to organise a strike?'

Mr. Hirst frowned at the chop on his plate.

'There are plenty of hot-heads at

Earnshaw's,' he said. 'As a matter of fact, it's not just pay that's the trouble. The strike would be more likely about being allowed to join a union.'

'Mr. Earnshaw would never consent to that!' Dick exclaimed.

'He might have to,' his father said. 'One thing Matthew Earnshaw would never be able to stomach would be a complete shut-down of his mill. And that could happen if there was a strike.'

'But how long would it last?' Dick asked. 'Without a union behind them the strikers would soon find themselves in difficulties. You can't feed hungry children on words, and that would be all the strikers would have to keep going on.'

'I thought strikers' wives and families could claim benefits,' Lucy put in. 'I read something about it in the paper the other day.'

'You forget that in most families in Lenthwaite both husband and wife work either at Earnshaw's or Murgatroyd's mills,' Dick pointed out, 'so both would be strikers if there was trouble. There'd be precious little money paid out by the authorities if a strike happened at Earnshaw's.'

'It's a big worry,' his father said shaking his greying head. 'I've talked to Ted Jackson and Clem Barraclough, who seem intent on trouble, but they call me a traitor to my own class. They say I'm years behind the times. They want a union at Earnshaw's and they mean to get it. In a way, I don't blame them. They're young men and they read the newspapers and listen to radio and T.V. They know what power the unions have when it comes to getting more money.'

'I still say they'll think twice before striking,' Dick persisted. 'They'll soon find which side their bread's buttered if they try anything on Matthew Earnshaw. If there's trouble I wouldn't put it past him to bring workpeople in from surrounding towns to keep his mill going. There's quite a lot of unemployment in the West Riding, especially in the textile trade.'

'It happened once before,' Mrs. Hirst said. 'You children are too young to remember it. I was a little girl at the time.' She shook her head. 'I pray God it never happens again.'

'Don't worry, Mum,' Dick reassured her 'I'm sure our people have too much sense to throw their livelihood away so foolishly.'

'Amen to that,' his father said fervently.

Lucy said nothing. She could have told them that more than one worker who had come to her department for attention during the past few days had wanted to talk about the subject that was at the back of all the Earnshaw employees' minds: the likelihood of trouble if Mr. Earnshaw did not increase their wages.

'We haven't had a rise for close on eighteen months,' one disgruntled weaver had said as Lucy bound up her sprained wrist. 'How do they think we can live with prices rising every day?'

'Well, sitting here talking about it won't drive it away,' Mrs. Hirst said with a little of her old briskness. 'If you've finished those chops you'd better have some pudding.'

'I'll get it,' Lucy said, jumping up. 'Just sit still, Mum. You're supposed to be taking it easy.'

As she served the treacle sponge to the two hungry men, she thought about the evening that lay before her.

That morning Mike had sought her out and once more asked her to go to the cinema with him.

'I'm a persistent sort of chap, Lucy,' he had said when she did not immediately accept his invitation. 'If you turn me down today I'll have another shot tomorrow. And so on and so on until you finally have to say Yes.'

She gave in then. In any case, going out for the evening with Mike attracted her. Since returning to Lenthwaite she had spent every evening at home. More than once her mother had urged her to go out and enjoy herself.

'You mustn't think you've to sit in every evening with me, lass,' Mrs. Hirst had said. 'Your dad rarely goes out, and there's always the T.V. to watch.'

Mike had said he would pick her up at half past six as the feature film started at a quarter past seven.

'Going out?' her mother said when, after washing up, she made for the door.

'Yes, I'm going to the cinema! In Bradford.'

'With Bessie?'

'No—with a young man!' Lucy's eyes twinkled.

'Nay, I don't believe it!' her mother cried while her father took his pipe out of his mouth as he looked up from his newspaper. 'Who is it—or aren't you telling?'

'It's Mike Earnshaw, if you must know!'

'Nay, wonder will never cease!' The boss's son! I don't suppose his father knows.'

'And why should it matter if he does?' Lucy asked sharply.

'No reason at all,' her mother replied drily. 'You're quite good enough for him.'

Exasperated, Lucy cried: 'I'm only going to the pictures with him, Mum, not getting engaged to the man.'

'Who said anything about getting engaged?' Mrs. Hirst demanded, then added quietly: 'Though you could do worse than marry the son of the richest man in the district.'

'Oh, Mum!' Lucy exploded.

Her mother's laughter followed her as she ran from the room and made for the stairs.

Mike arrived as the kitchen clock was striking seven.

Lucy, who had been waiting for the sound of his car, opened the door and went out to greet him. She noticed that curtains stirred in several houses around. It would soon be common knowledge that she had gone out for the evening with Mike Earnshaw!

She rather regretted she had not agreed to meet him somewhere in the town, perhaps outside the post office.

Then she frowned. Why had she always to be so on the defensive? Mike was taking her to the pictures. What did it matter if the whole of Lenthwaite knew?

'You look stunning,' Mike said.

His eyes shone as he leaned across to open the door on the passenger side for her to slip into the big car.

She was glad she had put on her new red coat which she had bought in London a month before but had never worn. It emphasised the slender lines of her figure and contrasted vividly with her very dark hair which she had had shampooed and set during her lunch hour.

Bradford, ten miles away, was soon reached. After parking the car Mike and Lucy walked to the cinema. It was a fine spring evening and Lucy suddenly felt very happy.

Since coming back to Lenthwaite she had

not been out in the evening. She had wanted to be with her mother. In any case there were few places to go for entertainment in a little mill town, Lenthwaite did not boast even a cinema.

Now she was happy, not only because her mother was so much better but also because she was in the company of a good-looking young man who obviously enjoyed being with her.

The film was excellent. The two young people came out into the lamp-lit streets when it was over.

'How about a drink before we go home?' Mike suggested, glancing at his watch: 'It's only just after ten. There's just time.'

But she shook her head.

'I'd rather not, Mike,' she said. 'Mother's sure to wait up for me, and she should be in bed.'

They walked through the lamp-lit streets back to the car. Occasionally they paused to look in a lighted shop window.

Mike had his arm linked through Lucy's. He brought her to a halt outside a furniture store.

'It must be fun setting up home,' he mused, looking at a comfortable three-piece suite, which occupied most of the window space.

'Why were you thinking of getting married?' she asked, a twinkle in her eyes.

He stole a glance at her.

'It depends on the girl,' he said. 'I haven't asked her yet.'

She did not know whether to be amused or annoyed.

Why did Mike say such things? Some girls might take him seriously. The disillusionment would come later when they discovered that he probably talked like this to all the girls he took out for the evening.

'Have you a girl in mind?' she smiled as they left the furniture shop behind.

'You know very well I have,' he said. 'I thought I'd made that pretty clear, Lucy.'

She looked at him curiously. This was not the voice of a man who was making fun of her. Then her heart quickened.

For the brown eyes in the strong face were filled with a longing, a hunger, she had never seen before in a man's glance. Not even Geoffrey Baines whom she had thought loved her.

She looked quickly away. Could it be possible that Mike really was falling in love with her?

Up to that moment she had thought that he was just attracted by a pretty face. Now she was not so sure.

They finished their walk to the car in silence. As they drove towards Lenthwaite Mike said, staring straight ahead at the moor road lit by the powerful headlights.

'It was love at first sight with me, Lucy! How do you feel about me?'

Yes! she thought. How did she feel about him? He attracted her. He was so good-looking, so full of life, so charming.

But was that enough? Until she knew him better she could not be sure.

'Oh, Mike, I'd rather not talk about it tonight,' she said. 'You see, I've not known you very long and—'

'I understand,' he said quietly. 'I'll say no more just now. But I'll ask you again when you've had time to think.'

As he spoke the headlights fell on a car standing at the side of the moor road. A slim figure stood beside it looking hopefully towards Mike's car as it approached.

'Why, that's Rosalind!' the young man muttered and applied the brakes.

The girl came towards them. Her fair hair shone in the headlights.

'Oh, Mike, am I glad to see you!' she cried, looking in through the window Lucy had wound down.

'What's up? A breakdown?' Mike asked.

'I've run out of petrol,' she replied. 'I feel such a fool. I knew I ought to have filled up before I left home but I was in a hurry and decided to risk it.'

'Better leave the car there till morning,' he said, 'then I'll send someone out with some petrol and tell them to bring the car back.

Hop in!'

As Lucy moved nearer to Mike to make room for the other girl Mike said:

'This is Lucy Hirst. I don't think you've met her, have you, Ros?'

The girl shook her head. Sitting beside Lucy she closed the door.

'I think you're Dick Hirst's sister, aren't you?' she asked, giving Lucy a curious look.

Lucy nodded wondering how Dick had become acquainted with this girl who, since her father died, had come into ownershp of Lenthwaite's other large mill. She hadn't known that he moved in circles where mink coats and expensive pearls were commonplace with the people who wore them.

'How do you come to be stranded on the moor at this time of night?' Mike asked.

'I've been to a drinks party at the Patons,' she replied, and with a little frown: 'Actually, I thought you'd have been there, Mike.'

She was disappointed he wasn't, Lucy thought and wondered if the girl beside her was in love with Mike.

'I was invited but I thought I'd give the party a miss and take Lucy out instead,' Mike said.

'You didn't miss anything,' Rosalind said. 'The Patons are the most boring people but—well, they are one of Murgatroyd's biggest customers so it was up to me to accept their invitation.'

'The Patons are Bradford merchants,' Mike said for Lucy's benefit. 'They buy cloth from both Murgatroyds and Earnshaws. I take it my father was there, Ros?'

'Yes! He offered me a lift back but I told him I'd have to drive my car back as I'd taken it. He seemed surprised you weren't there, Mike.'

Mike gave a short laugh in which there was little humour.

'I'm sure of it,' he said and fell silent.

Rosalind asked Lucy how she liked being back in Lenthwaite after living so long in London.

'I like it very well,' she replied, then added: 'You know, I suppose, that I'm working at Earnshaw's mill—as a nurse?'

'Yes, Dick told me. He also said your mother had been ill. I do hope she's better now.'

'Yes, she's improved a lot in the last few days.'

In the light from the dashboard Lucy stole a glance at Mike's face. His usually smiling mouth was set in a grim almost forbidding line.

She wondered if he had been hoping to say more to her on the subject they had been discussing before they saw Rosalind at the side of the road.

True, he had said he would not press her further that night; but Mike was a mercurial unpredictable character. It was very probable that, in spite of his promise, he would have made one more effort to convince her that he loved her.

Before entering Lenthwaite Mike swung the car between a pair of white gateposts and up a winding drive to a square built house, which looked out over pleasant lawns to a small lake.

'I hope you'll both come in for some coffee,' Rosalind invited.

Mike hesitated; but Lucy shook her head.

'I'd rather get home, Miss Murgatroyd, thank you,' she said. 'My mother won't settle until I return.'

'Very well,' the girl said, hiding her disappointment.

It was obvious to Lucy that if she could have detained Mike she would have done.

They dropped Rosalind at the house then turned in the drive and returned to the main road.

'Poor Ros,' Mike said. 'I feel sorry for her having to go on living in that morgue of a house all by herself. Except for the servants, that is,' he added.

'Couldn't she get something smaller?'

He shrugged. 'She seems to think her father would have expected it of her. The Murgatroyds have lived at Stanfield Hall for over a hundred years, ever since Ros's grandfather founded the business and built the house.'

They drove into Lenthwaite. As he drew up outside Lucy's door Mike said:

'Think over what I said, Lucy. I really meant it.'

She got out of the car and smiled back at him.

'Thank you for a lovely evening, Mike,' she said, then before he could say any more, she turned on her heel and went into the house.

# PART THREE

# THE MANAGER

## CHAPTER NINE

Rosalind Murgatroyd looked round the big office. Her eyes were unhappy.

If only her father was still alive, she thought. He would have known what to do. But he was dead. She had to solve this crisis on her own.

She looked up as a knock came at the door. She drew a deep breath. Now for it!

'Come in!' she called.

The man who entered was in his thirties. He had a bright breezy manner and smiled at Rosalind as he crossed the office towards her.

'You wanted to see me, Miss Murgatroyd?' he said.

'Yes, Mr. Taylor. I've just had a visit from Mr. Helliwell, our accountant.'

He frowned as if puzzled. Rather nervously the tip of his finger went to the little fair moustache which decorated his upper lip. His dark eyes were wary now.

'I'm not quite sure I understand—' he said.

Rosalind drew a deep breath.

'The accountants have just finished the

104

annual audit of the firm's books,' she said quietly. 'Mr. Helliwell tells me there are certain irregularities—'

'Irregularities, Miss Murgatroyd!' He sounded shocked.

'Yes, Mr. Taylor, irregularities! The stock list taken six months ago does not agree with today's stock in hand allowing for sales. Some cloth has been disposed of which has not been entered in the books. Do you know anything about it, Mr. Taylor?'

He shook his head. There was a look of deep concern on his rather narrow face now.

'I'm as mystified as you must be, Miss Murgatroyd,' he said. 'I suppose you are quite sure that the accountants have not made some mistake?'

'Oh, they haven't made a mistake, Mr. Taylor,' she said firmly. 'The person who made the mistake is the one who has been disposing of Murgatroyd cloth without entering the sale in the proper place.'

'But that means!—'

'Yes, Mr. Taylor, that means that someone has been defrauding the company over quite a long period. Of course, it won't be easy to prove but—'

'I'll look into it at once!' he cried.

'I think you'd better,' she said drily. 'If you don't come up with a satisfactory answer I shall have to inform the police.'

He swallowed. She saw the Adam's apple

in his rather scraggy throat jump up and down.

'Oh, I don't think this is a matter for such drastic action,' he exclaimed. 'I'm sure your father wouldn't have—'

'My father would have telephoned the police the minute he was told of the accountants' suspicions and well you know it, Mr. Taylor.' Suddenly she felt ice cold, well able to handle this man. He had thought he only had a girl to deal with, did he? Well, she'd show him.

'Of course, it won't be too easy proving anything against anyone,' he said after staring at her in silence for a few seconds. 'No invoices, no transport records, nothing.'

'Yet the cloth left the mill, probably at night. Someone may have seen it moved.'

'I doubt it! Whoever embarked on anything like that would be a fool to do it in front of witnesses, Miss Murgatroyd.'

'Well, you'd better make some enquiries, Mr. Taylor. If you don't come up with a satisfactory answer I shall telephone the police this afternoon and they'll start their own investigation.'

'Very well!' There was a stoop to his shoulders as he walked to the door. Before he left the room he looked back: 'I think we can sort this out by ourselves Miss Murgatroyd. No need to call in the law.'

She said nothing and, after a few seconds,

he turned and went away.

She realised suddenly that she was trembling.

'He knows I suspect him,' she thought. 'Oh, why had it to happen at all? What are a few bolts of cloth to the upheaval that will be caused if the police come? But Mr. Helliwell was emphatic. I wouldn't wonder if he doesn't send for them himself if I don't.'

She got up from her seat and began to pace up and down the office. She felt so lonely, so—so friendless. If only she had someone to turn to for advice!

She thought of Mike. Her heart was sad. If only Mike had loved her as she loved him. Once they had been childhood sweethearts; but when Mike had been sent away to school, and had later gone to university, he had grown away from her.

When he had returned to Lenthwaite and had taken up his work in his father's mill, he had soon let her know that so far as he was concerned, they could only ever be friends. Nothing more.

'Yet friends should help each other in a crisis,' she thought; then turned and looked across at the telephone on the desk as it began to ring.

'Yes?' she asked, picking up the receiver.

The girl on the switchboard told her that Mr. Michael Earnshaw would like a word with her. Her heart quickened. How amazing that the man she loved should ring her up just when she was thinking about him!

'Hello, Mike,' she said when the operator put him through.

'Hi, Ros!' he said. 'I thought you'd like to know I sent someone out to recover your car. They rang up from the garage to say they've taken it to the Hall and put it away in the garage.'

'Thanks very much, Mike,' she said gratefully. In the stress of the events of that morning she'd forgotten that she'd run out of petrol on the moor last evening. A car from the mill had picked her up as usual to take her to the office at nine o'clock.

'Mike,' she said, sensing that he might be going to ring off. 'Can you spare me a quarter of an hour this morning?'

'Why, yes, Ros, I suppose so! What is it about?'

'I'd rather wait till I see you. How about having coffee with me at Ann's Pantry in ten minutes?'

'All right! In ten minutes!'

She heard the receiver click at the other end of the line and replaced her own with a sigh. Mike didn't seem any too enthusiastic at being asked to take time off on what might be a very busy morning for him.

She went down to the mill yard. Rawlings, the mill chauffeur, was polishing the car. When he was not driving Rosalind he drove one of the firm's vans.

'Oh, Rawlings, run me into Lenthwaite, will you?' Rosalind asked.

'Certainly, Miss!' He was a kindly middle-aged man who had been with Murgatroyd's for twenty years. 'I'll just get my jacket.'

She sat in the back of the big limousine. So often she had seen her father sitting where she was sitting now, Rawlings at the wheel. The weight of her responsibilities pressed down on her. She had never wanted to run a mill employing hundreds of people. All she had ever wanted was to be married to Mike and bring up a big family.

Rawlings dropped her at Ann's Pantry. 'Wait for me,' she said. 'I shan't be long.'

Mike was not there. She seated herself at a corner table and ordered coffee. Presently Mike arrived.

'Got held up by a phone call just as I was leaving,' he apologised, then looking into her white face: 'What is it, Ros? You look quite upset.'

She was spared a reply as the waitress came up to take their order. When he turned to her again she forced a smile.

'I want your advice, Mike,' she said. 'It's about Mr. Taylor, my manager.'

'Eddie Taylor?' He frowned. 'What's he been up to?'

'I'm not sure that he's been up to anything

at all,' she said. 'It's just that—well, the accountants have found something out—'

'And you think Taylor's at the bottom of it?'

She told him what Mr. Helliwell had said about the cloth that had disappeared, the discrepancy in the stock book.

'I talked to Mr. Taylor and he promised to look into things,' she said. 'He as good as begged me not to send for the police, which Mr. Helliwell seems to think I should do.'

'And so do I!' he exclaimed, his eyes flashing. 'Why, that man Taylor's a crook. You've only got to look at him to know that. How your father put up with him, I'll never know.'

'It will be very hard to prove anything against him! The cloth's gone—there's no doubt about that—but half a dozen people could have come back in the night and taken it. It must have been going on for a long time for so much to disappear.'

He put his hand over hers.

'Ros, all the people at Murgatroyd's who could have been concerned in this business have been with the firm since they left school. They wouldn't steal cloth from you. They're too loyal, too honest. They thought the world of your father. They probably think the same about you.'

'Then what do you think I ought to do?'

'Tell the police. Have a proper enquiry

110

made. If Taylor's innocent he has nothing to fear. If he's guilty then—well, he'll get his deserts.'

'And if they can't find anything out?'

'Then you're no worse off than you are now. But whatever else you do you must make an excuse for getting rid of Eddie Taylor. He's a rotten apple in a good barrel.'

'I said I'd give Mr. Taylor until this afternoon to look into things.'

'I shouldn't let that worry you. Let's go to the police station together, Ros—now!'

But she wouldn't. 'I gave him my word. I'll wait until this afternoon.'

'Would you like me to come back to the mill with you?'

But she shook her head. She smiled faintly.

'No, thanks, I'd rather you stayed out of it for the moment, Mike,' she said, then warmly: 'But thank you for letting me talk to you. It's nice to know I've got such a good friend.'

'We'll always be that, Ros,' he said and gave her hand another squeeze.

They left the café together. As Rosalind got into the waiting car Mike said:

'Ring me later when you know more,' he said, then stood staring after the old Daimler as it was driven away.

Later that afternoon, as she had heard nothing from Eddie Taylor, Rosalind rang his office.

'He's not here, Miss Murgatroyd,' his secretary said.

'Is he somewhere about the mill?'

'I don't think so.' The girl sounded a little uncertain. 'I saw him driving out of the mill yard about half an hour ago. He didn't tell me where he was going before he left.'

Rosalind returned the receiver to its rest. She felt uneasy. Where could her general manager have been going at half past three in the afternoon without telling his secretary?

His job was running the mill, not careering about in his car in the middle of a working day.

Her uneasiness grew during the next hour. At last she could bear the suspense no longer. Jumping up she made for the door. Two minutes later she was entering the General Office.

'Has Mr. Taylor returned yet?' she asked his secretary, who had got up from her typewriter as she entered the office.

'I'm afraid not, Miss Murgatroyd,' the girl said.

Rosalind realised that the other girls in the room had broken off from their work to listen.

'You'd better come with me into his room,' she said and, followed by his secretary, she led the way into Eddie Taylor's office.

'I think you said he didn't tell you where he was going?' Rosalind asked the girl.

'No, Miss Murgatroyd. He just said he didn't think he'd be back today as he went out, that's all I know.'

As Rosalind looked at the tidy desk the girl suddenly said:

'He was carrying a bag with him, Miss Murgatroyd.'

'What sort of bag?' Rosalind asked.

'A sort of suitcase. It seemed heavy for he leaned to one side as he carried it.'

Rosalind's heart sank. What did this mean? That Eddie Taylor had gone for good? It was beginning to look like it.

'All right, Tessie, you can go back to your work,' she said.

The girl, as if relieved, turned on her heel and disappeared.

Rosalind crossed to the big desk. Except for some mill stationery its drawers were empty.

She crossed to the filing cabinet against one of the walls. Several files had been removed from this. She was sure. The safe, standing against another wall, was unlocked. Only a few days before she had been standing by Eddie Taylor's side as he had looked up something for her in one of the ledgers.

Only two of the six ledgers remained. The other four must have gone with him.

She wondered how he had hoped to get away with it.

Perhaps he hadn't. It was only because the

audit had been finished ahead of time that he had been caught out. No doubt he had meant to take off in the next day or two in any case just before the accountants reported.

Once abroad with the money he must have been accumulating over the past year he would disappear, perhaps for ever.

Mr. Helliwell had not told her how much money was involved, but it must have been a great deal for Eddie Taylor to think it was worth leaving the country for.

She shut the safe door and the filing cabinet drawers then left the office. Tessie Bates watched her go past her desk and said afterwards that Miss Murgatroyd's face was as white as a ghost's.

Rosalind went back to her own office and picked up the telephone.

'Get Mr. Helliwell at Helliwell, Cartwright's, the accountants,' she told the operator; then when Mr. Helliwell answered: 'Could you come round, Mr. Helliwell? It's very important.'

'Can't it wait until morning?' he asked. She could almost see him frowning.

'I'm afraid not. I'm going to do what you advised—and I'd like you to be here when the police come.'

'Very well!' he said with a sigh. 'I'll come at once.'

He was as good as his word. Ten minutes later she was ringing the local police station.

She and Mr. Helliwell sat in silence until Rosalind's secretary announced that Inspector Madden had arrived.

'Show him in,' Rosalind said, then braced herself for the coming ordeal.

Later that evening Mike rang her. She was eating a solitary meal in the big dining room at Stansfield Hall. She hurried to the telephone.

'Well, anything happen after you left me?' he asked.

She told him. He whistled.

'Just as I told you, Taylor's a crook!' he exclaimed. 'I suppose they'll be looking out for him.'

She frowned. 'I don't know, Mike. Inspector Madden wasn't at all helpful.'

'How do you mean?' he demanded indignantly. 'Surely the police will arrest Taylor when they catch up with him.'

'It isn't as easy as that,' she said. 'The inspector said we'd have to have proof that Mr. Taylor is guilty before they can arrest him. And of course we've no proof at all. He took pretty good care to cover his tracks.'

'Then he could get well out of the country before the police will move?'

'It looks like it! In fact, he could be anywhere by this time. His car was found at Manchester Airport half an hour ago. Inspector Madden rang to let me know.'

'But it's fantastic. He could get away with

it!'

'I suppose so! As a matter of fact, I rather hope he does. At least it saves me from having to sack him.'

'And what will you do now?' he asked. 'You can't run a great business like Murgatroyd's on your own, Ros.'

'I suppose I'll have to find someone else to take Taylor's place,' she said, a note of weariness in her voice.

'I wish I could help,' he said awkwardly, then after telling her to keep her chin up, he rang off and she went back to her lonely supper.

Mike told his father and mother what had happened as they took coffee together after their evening meal.

Mr. Earnshaw heard him out in silence as he puffed at his cigar.

'I only hope she gets the right sort of chap to run the business,' Mike said in conclusion. 'A girl like Rosalind is a sitting target for rogues like Eddie Taylor.'

'She's already got the right sort of chap to run her business for her,' Mr. Earnshaw said, and Mike and his mother looked at him curiously.

'What do you mean, Dad?' Mike asked. 'She hasn't had time to find anyone yet.'

'She doesn't need to look further than this house,' his father replied complacently. 'Tomorrow morning I shall offer her your

116

services, lad. You'll be the General Manager of Murgatroyd's until such time as Rosalind finds someone suitable. It's the least we can do for her in her hour of need.'

But there was a look on his face that told Mike there was more in this than met the eye.

# CHAPTER TEN

'Can I see you tonight, Lucy!' Mike sounded excited.

'I don't know, Mike,' she replied. 'I have quite a lot to do in the house when I get home and—'

'Please, Lucy! I must see you!'

She stood there, worried and uncertain, the telephone receiver in her hand. Why had Mike telephoned her like this when he could so easily have walked down from his office to talk to her?

She wondered why he sounded so excited. What could have happened to get him so worked up since she had seen him two evenings before?

'You will meet me, won't you, Lucy?' he asked impatiently when she did not reply.

'If it's so important I suppose I must,' she said.

'It's certainly important—to both of us!' he declared. 'I'll pick you up at seven o'clock.'

As she replaced the receiver in its rest, and went back into the next room to finish binding up a cut hand for one of the weavers, she wondered why it was so urgent that she should see Mike that evening. What had he meant about it being important to both of them?

She remembered how, on the way back from Bradford, he had told her he loved her, had said he would give her time to think over what he had said.

He was an impatient young man. Perhaps he was not prepared to wait for his answer any longer.

Yet as she went about her work for the rest of the day, Lucy could not help but feel that there was something else, something she did not know about and which Mike felt she should hear.

He picked her up promptly at seven o'clock. He drove out of Lenthwaite and up the moor road until they reached a point where they had an extensive view of the surrounding countryside.

Pulling the car off the road Mike turned to his passenger.

'Quite a lot has happened since I saw you two days ago,' he said.

She frowned, puzzled. What did he mean?

'I don't understand,' she murmured.

'I'm not working at my father's mill just now,' he said. 'I'm Rosalind Murgatroyd's manager!'

She stared at him in amazement. How could he possibly be Rosalind's manager when her business and his father's were such competitors?

He told her then about the missing cloth and how Eddie Taylor had vanished.

'That left Ros without a manager so my father decided I would fill the bill nicely.' There was a hint of bitterness in his voice. 'So this morning I started in on my new job.'

'I suppose your father thought he owed it to Miss Murgatroyd to offer to help,' Lucy said. 'I don't suppose it would have been easy to find another manager at such short notice.'

He shook his head. His eyes flashed.

'If you think that, Lucy, you don't know my father,' he exclaimed. 'No! it's always been his fondest ambition that Ros and I should marry and unite the two businesses. I've told him over and over again that I don't love Ros, but he's kept at me. Now, by thrusting me into this situation, he thinks he'll bring things to a head. He's hoping I'll see how well the two businesses could run in partnership, and if I'm seeing Ros day in and day out, I'll finally ask her to marry me. But I won't oblige him! I jolly well won't!'

He thrust out his lower lip. She nearly laughed. He looked exactly like a sulky schoolboy.

Then he turned to her, a new light in his

eyes. He took her hand.

'I told you I loved you the other night,' he said. 'I asked you to tell me how you felt when you'd had time to think things over. Have you got an answer for me yet?'

'Oh, Mike, I like you very much but—well, I'm not sure that I love you,' she said in a low voice.

He did not seem to hear her. His grip on her hand tightened.

'Something else has happened since I saw you last,' he went on and there was excitement in his voice now. 'About a month ago I wrote to a man I know in London. He's connected with an agency that places people in suitable jobs. I told him how keen I was on salesmanship and explained that my father wouldn't give me a chance in this direction.

'This came this morning,' he said, feeling in an inside pocket and holding out a piece of headed notepaper. The address was THE SLOANE SALES AGENCY, Sloane Square, London. S.W.1.

'Dear Mr. Earnshaw (she read). Re your earlier letter. An opportunity has come up with the Textile Rollings Co. Ltd. for a representative to tour the southern counties on their behalf—by helicopter. Perhaps you will contact me by telephone as there is some urgency about the matter. I can give you details of salary and other items of interest when I hear from you.

Yours sincerely,
Sidney Dell
Director.'

Lucy handed the letter back with a puzzled frown.

'But what does this mean, Mike?' she asked. 'You've just been given the job of manager of Murgatroyd's yet you're considering taking another job—in London. And why should it matter whether or not you can pilot a helicopter?'

He grinned. 'It's a gimmick, a rather clever one, I think. Salesmen are two a penny—but a salesman who arrives to talk to a prospective client by helicpter rather than by car is going to have a tremendous pull. No sales director is going to turn such a man away without at least seeing him. Sidney Dell of the Agency was tickled pink when I put the idea to him. My experience in textiles helped, of course, but I think it was the 'copter that did the trick!'

His eyes glowed as they looked into hers.

'Don't you see, Lucy?' he cried. 'This is my chance to escape from Lenthwaite to a job I know I could do well. What I want you to tell me is whether or not you love me enough to go with me and share my life.'

Her heart quickened. What did he mean?

121

Was he proposing to her? Was he inviting her to marry him and go with him to this new job he had been offered?

She looked into his good-looking face. He was handsome and charming, and he had the qualities which would probably make him a success in this job he had been offered. In fact, most girls would consider themselves lucky to have such a young man in love with them as Mike obviously was in love with her.

Yet she could not make up her mind. She liked him; but was liking enough?

'We could be married in London,' he said. 'Without the sort of fuss there'd be if we tried to get married in Lenthwaite.'

She knew what he meant by 'fuss'. He knew very well what Mr. Earnshaw would say if a hint that he was in love with the daughter of one of his workpeople reached his ears.

'Would you tell your mother and father about us?' she asked.

'Only by letter when you became my wife.' He chuckled. 'I'd love to see the Old Man's face when my letter reached him. It would just pay him out for trying to rush me into—other things.'

She frowned. 'I don't like the sound of that, Mike. You make it seem as if you'd be marrying me just to spite your father.'

Instantly he was all remorse. He took her hand again and put it to his lips.

'I didn't mean it like that, Lucy!' he cried.

'I swear I didn't. It's just that—well, he's bullied me all my life. It would be nice to feel for once that I was on top.'

Quietly she said:

'I won't be rushed into this, Mike. I like you—I've said so before—but I'm not sure that I love you.'

'But I must know! They won't keep the London job open for me indefinitely.'

'Then why don't you take it—without me? You may not like it. If you don't I suppose you'll return to Lenthwaite. I'll still be here. Your going away might help me to make up my mind, so that, when you come back—'

His brows came down in a scowl.

'You're making excuses, Lucy. I don't want putting off. I want you to go to London with me so we can be married there.'

But she wouldn't be rushed.

'You forget I have responsibilities, Mike,' she said. 'My mother isn't well. I just can't walk out on her as you apparently want me to. And this new job I've taken at Earnshaw's. A fine daughter-in-law your father would think me if I threw up the job and went off with you when he's depending on you to carry the mill on when he retires. I can see him blaming me for talking you into taking this London job.'

'I'm not bothered about what my father thinks,' he muttered. 'I'm sorry it will mean leaving your mother, but after all she still has

123

your father and your brother left to care for her.'

She shook her head firmly.

'No, Mike, I can't do it,' she said. 'I promised two days ago that I'd give you an answer one way or the other. Well, I've just made up my mind. I refuse to be rushed. If you won't give me more time the answer is No.'

He tried to argue with her, but she was adamant. At last she said:

'Take me home, Mike. There's no point in talking like this.'

Pettishly, he flung away from her and started the engine. Swinging the car back on the road he drove recklessly towards Lenthwaite. He said nothing further but the black look on his face gave away the fury behind his thoughts.

Lucy slept little that night. Over and over again she went over in her mind all that Mike had said to her and what she had replied.

Her thoughts went to that other man in London who, for a short time, had laid claim to her heart. Perhaps her experience with him had made her over cautious in her relationship with Mike Earnshaw. Was it possible that if she had never known, never loved, Geoffrey Baines, she might have come under Mike's spell, have thought herself in love with him and been happy to become his wife?

She tossed and turned in bed, her thoughts in a turmoil.

At last she could lie there no longer. She got up and walked up and down the little room.

She crossed to the dressing table and glanced at her watch. It was nearly half-past two!

'I'll go down and make a cup of tea,' she thought. 'It might help me to get to sleep.'

She crept downstairs and into the kitchen. A dying glow from the sinking fire greeted her. She put a few sticks of firewood on the embers and was rewarded by a cheerful blaze.

As she waited for the kettle to boil she thought she heard a sound on the stairs. She looked towards the door.

Her mother came into the room, a thin frail figure. She gave Lucy a faint smile.

'Couldn't you sleep, either?' she asked. 'I heard you moving about and decided to come down and join you.'

'You ought to be in bed,' Lucy frowned. 'Even if you can't sleep, you'd be resting.'

Mrs. Hirst did not speak but seated herself before the fire holding her dressing gown tightly about her thin form.

Lucy brewed the tea in silence then poured a cup for her mother then one for herself.

'Thanks, love!' Mrs. Hirst murmured, then looking at her daughter over the rim of the cup: 'It's not like you to lie awake at

125

night.'

Lucy smiled. 'It does happen sometimes!'

Her mother nodded.

'It's that young man, isn't it?' she asked. 'I thought you looked upset when you came in after leaving him. Had you had a fall out?'

Lucy shook her head.

'No! All that happened was that he asked me to marry him and go away from Lenthwaite.'

'And you turned him down, eh?'

'He's been offered a job in London. It would mean leaving his father's firm. He wanted me to go with him.'

Her mother said nothing but stared into the flames, cup in hand.

'I feel all mixed up, Mum,' Lucy said. 'I like him but do I love him? I can't be sure.'

'It would be a wonderful match,' Mrs. Hirst murmured. 'Even if he does take this job in London he's his father's heir. Sooner or later he'd give up the job and come back. Why, he'd be throwing away a fortune if he deserted his father and never returned to Lenthwaite.'

'Are you saying I ought to marry him because he'll be rich one day, Mum?' Lucy demanded.

Her mother put her empty cup down. She looked up at Lucy with unhappy eyes.

'I'm thinking what's best for you, love,' she said in a low voice. 'You see, when your dad

126

and me were married we had a very poor time of it at first. Things were bad in the textile world and wages were low. Oh, your dad kept his job at Earnshaw's when other men were laid off. But I was always fearful that one day he would come in and say he was out of work. Insecurity—fear of being on the dole—make you cautious, Lucy. They make you want better things for your children than you had for yourself.'

'But things are different today, Mum! I have a good job, in any case. I would have to give that up if I married Mike.'

'But surely you don't want to go on for thirty years and more like Nurse Bailey. You're young, love. Life lies all before you. Don't you want a home of your own, bairns, perhaps?'

Suddenly to her complete amazement Lucy burst into tears. When her mother held out her arms she went on her knees before the older woman and, burying her face in the other's lap, cried as if her heart was breaking.

'There, there, love! It's going to be all right. I know it is.'

Presently Lucy lifted a tear-streaked face and looked up at her mother.

'I'm sorry, Mum,' she said. 'I oughtn't to have given way like that. It's just that—well, sometimes things get on top of you and you let go!'

Her mother nodded then bent forward to

kiss her.

'I know it, love, I know it! And now, go back to bed. And stop worrying about that young man. It will all work out right in the end, I'm sure of it.'

Lucy got to her feet. She smiled as she wiped her eyes.

'It's done me good to talk to you, Mum. It was always like that when I was a child.' She kissed the top of her mother's head. 'Come to bed, Mum. You look tired out.'

But her mother shook her head.

'I'll come up later,' she said. 'I like it here by the fire. Goodnight, love!'

Lucy, hesitating for a second or two more, made for the door. When she looked back her mother was staring into the fire oblivious of everything but her own thoughts.

## CHAPTER ELEVEN

It had been a long tiring day. Lucy, making a pot of tea for Dr. Tolson and herself, thought of the stream of young people who, all that day, had come to the First Aid department to be examined by the medical officer.

Matthew Earnshaw and Co. Ltd., with a full order book, was recruiting new labour not only in Lenthwaite but also from the district around. It did not fit in with Mr.

Earnshaw's views that he should have even one loom standing idle.

Most of these new employees were teenagers and had to be seen by the doctor before taking up their work in the mill. They would then be instructed in their new duties by an older weaver until they were able to take on a loom single handed.

'You look tired!'

Alan Tolson took the cup of tea from Lucy. She smiled.

'It's been a tiring sort of day,' she said.

She did not tell him she had slept badly. He would not be interested. Why should he? She meant nothing to him except someone who happened to work with him twice a week at the mill.

He finished his tea and stood up.

'I'd better be on my way,' he said. 'I've a couple of calls to make yet. They're not urgent or I would have made them this morning before I came here.'

They both heard the hooter signalling the end of the day, then the rush of feet as the workpeople raced across the mill yard eager to get home.

'Well, goodnight, Nurse,' the young doctor said; but before she could reply the telephone rang.

Lucy lifted the receiver. An agitated voice asked:

'Is Dr. Tolson with you?'

'Why, yes. He's just leaving,' she replied.

'Put him on, will you? This is the police.'

She turned to Alan.

'The police want you,' she said, and, with a frown, he took the receiver from her.

'Yes, yes, I understand,' Lucy heard him mutter. 'The Hollins cross roads. Yes! I'll come at once.'

He turned to Lucy.

'There's been a car smash at the crossroads,' he said. 'I'll have to go at once. Several people injured.'

As he made for the door she said:

'I'll come with you. You may need help!'

He shook his head with a frown.

'There's no need! You've done a long day's work—'

'There's no time to argue,' she said. 'Let's go!'

His grey eyes met hers, saw the determination in them, then with a shrug, he led the way from the room, bag in hand.

His car was in the mill yard. The last of the workers were streaming through the gates as Alan Tolson—Lucy by his side—drove his car into the street.

As they drove at a fast rate out of the town Lucy heard an ambulance bell and a police siren somewhere ahead. They reached the scene of the accident to find a car overturned on the grass verge at the far side of the cross roads. Another car, which had obviously tried

130

to avoid a collision with the first, had slewed round and was now facing back the way it had come.

Three people had been lifted out of the car which had overturned and been laid on the grass. A man and woman—plainly shocked by what had happened but otherwise uninjured—were standing by the side of the other car.

When Alan and Lucy appeared a policeman made toward them. His hand was raised to stop them.

'You mustn't come this way, sir,' he began, then recognising the doctor: 'Oh, good evening, Doctor. I didn't see it was you!'

'Anyone badly hurt, Sergeant?' Alan asked.

'One man's unconscious; the other two seem more dazed than anything else.'

Alan drew up at the side of the road and he and Lucy jumped out.

'Better go and get those two people over there into an ambulance,' Alan, said, nodding towards the man and woman standing by the car in the middle of the road. 'They need treatment for shock. I can see that from here.'

As Alan turned away Lucy made for the couple standing in the road.

The woman was crying. Tears were pouring down her faded cheeks. She looked about sixty, Lucy decided. The man was a little older. He was trembling violently.

'It wasn't my fault, I swear it wasn't!' he

131

kept saying over and over again. 'He came into the roundabout at a fast rate as I was going round it.' He pointed with a shaking finger. 'Look, Nurse, you can see the two white lines. He should have waited behind those till I was safely past. But he didn't. When he saw he was going to hit me he wrenched his wheel over and went on his side. I swerved to miss him and finished up facing the way I'd come.'

'Very well, sir!' Lucy said soothingly. 'Here are two ambulancemen. They'll take you to the hospital and give you something for the shock you've suffered.'

'But the car!' the woman sobbed. 'What will happen to the car? And Patty! We were going to visit my niece, Patty. She'll be expecting us.'

Lucy with the help of the ambulance attendants got the old couple into the ambulance. Lucy sighed as they were driven away.

Then she turned and made towards the little group at the side of the road where Alan Tolson was kneeling beside the unconscious man.

'He's bleeding badly,' he said as she came up. 'We'll have to put a tourniquet on then get him to hospital without any delay.'

They worked quickly, oblivious of those around them. When the tourniquet had been applied to the bleeding leg the ambulance men took over and put the casualty into their vehicle.

Alan and Lucy turned their attention to the other passengers of the overturned car. One was a young boy; the other his mother and the wife of the driver.

The woman was dazed from a blow on the head. Alan examined her and the look he gave Lucy told her that he suspected a fracture of the skull. The boy had hurt his back and was sobbing quietly. The woman lay still though her eyes were wide open as she stared up into the blue sky.

After the doctor's examination the ambulance men took over. Alan spoke briefly to the police inspector who had now arrived with other policemen from Lenthwaite. Already photographs of the incident and measurements of the skid marks were being taken.

'Let's go!' he said at last to Lucy. 'I'd like to go to the hospital to see what's going on. I didn't like the look of the man. He'd lost a lot of blood. They'll have to set up a transfusion without delay. I'd also like to see the woman's X-rays later.'

They drove back to the little town and soon were drawing up outside the canopied entrance to the hospital. Alan had offered to take Lucy home first but she had said she preferred to go with him to see how their patients were progressing.

They found that the man had recovered consciousness. The young casualty officer smiled at Alan.

'Your tourniquet saved him, Doctor,' he said. 'When I've got him stitched up I'll go over him. There might be other things we haven't found yet.'

'How did he come to cut his leg?' Lucy asked, curious.

'He had a bottle in his pocket. When he was thrown from the car it broke and a jagged piece severed an artery.'

'And his wife?' Alan asked.

'I've sent her down for an X-ray. I'll know something very soon.'

Alan and Lucy went to talk to the other three victims of the accident. The boy was sucking a glucose sweet one of the nurses had given him. The man and woman from the other car were sitting beside him drinking sweet tea.

'How are you all feeling?' Alan asked.

The boy did not reply but there were tears in his eyes and his lips trembled. The man and woman said they felt all right and wanted to go.

'It's Patty, my niece, we're worried about,' the woman said. 'She's expecting us. She'll begin to worry when we don't turn up.'

'Is she on the telephone?' Alan asked.

'Oh, yes,' the woman replied proudly. 'She and her husband have always had a telephone, ever since they were married.'

'Then I'm sure one of the nurses will telephone her to say you've been delayed—if you know the number,' Alan said.

'I have it here!' The woman—whose name was Knowles—opened a capacious handbag and produced a slip of paper. 'That's it! Say we'll be there as soon as we can, nurse.'

She handed the paper to Lucy. Alan, catching her eye, winked.

She went off to find a telephone and soon got through to Mrs. Knowles's niece. When she returned to Casualty Mrs. Knowles thanked her profusely.

A policeman was sitting with Mr. Knowles taking his statement.

'Came across the white lines on to the roundabout as I was driving round it,' Lucy heard the old man say indignantly.

She went across to Alan who was talking to the Casualty Officer. He smiled as she approached.

'They've just telephoned from X-ray,' he said. 'There's no sign of a fracture. It'll just turn out to be concussion, I suppose. The woman's lucky!'

After Alan had talked to the policeman for a couple of minutes, he and Lucy went out to his car.

'Thanks for all your help,' Alan said as they drove into the town.

'It was nothing,' she exclaimed. 'I'm only

glad I was able to help at all, and that everything went so well.'

They had to pass his house. Lucy said as they approached it:

'You can put me down at your gate and I'll walk the rest of the way home. It's not far.'

He said nothing to this but when they reached the entrance to the drive which ran up to the old house he asked:

'Will you come in and meet my daughter, Lucy?' Then when she hesitated he said quickly: 'I hope you don't mind my calling you Lucy when we're off duty.'

She smiled. 'Of course I don't. And I'd love to meet your daughter. I mustn't stay long, though. My mother will be wondering where I am.'

'Have any of your neighbours a phone?' he asked as he turned into the drive and drove up to the house.

'Yes, Bessie Shaw, my friend. She's Mr. Earnshaw's secretary and he had the phone put in so he could telephone her whenever he felt like it. I'm not too sure that Bessie liked the idea when it was put to her.'

'Then I'll telephone her and ask her to go over to tell your mother where you are and that you'll be home soon.'

They went into the house. A door to one side of the big square hall flew open and a small girl charged across the tiled floor to throw herself into her father's arms.

Alan kissed her warmly then smiled at Lucy.

'This is Margy,' he said, and to the little girl: 'This is Nurse Hirst. Say hello to her.'

The merry little face under the fair curls was raised to Lucy. The blue eyes twinkled mischievously.

'Hello, Nursie!' she chuckled, then before her father could stop her, she whirled away and made for the stairs.

They watched her scramble up to the first floor and disappear. Alan sighed.

'She's quite a handful,' he said. 'The trouble is she's too much on her own. Mrs. Barrett, my housekeeper, is very good with her, but she's an old woman and has the housework to do. She can't really handle a lively child as well.'

He led the way into a pleasant sitting room where a cheerful fire burned. The furniture was shabby but comfortable. A telephone stood on an occasional table near the window and the young doctor crossed to it.

'Do you know your friend's number?' he asked.

She gave it to him and he picked up the receiver. As he was making the call his housekeeper came into the room. She smiled at Lucy and waited until Alan turned away from the telephone.

'Have there been any calls, Mrs. Barrett?' Alan asked.

137

'Mrs. Tempest rang about her backache,' the old woman replied. 'I told her you'd call tomorrow morning.'

'You didn't tell her to take a couple of aspirins, by any chance?'

'As a matter fact, I did!' Mrs. Barrett snorted. 'Silly old woman! There's nothing really wrong with her. She just likes to be a nuisance.'

'Anything else?'

'No, I'm glad to say.' She looked at Lucy then back to her employer. 'What about your supper, doctor? There's plenty—if the young lady's minded to stay.'

He raised his eyebrows at Lucy. She frowned.

'Oh, I really shouldn't—' she began, but he shook his head.

'Your mother won't be expecting you back now,' he said. 'Margy and I would enjoy your company.'

'But your evening surgery?'

'This is my evening off. Morning surgery only on Thursdays.'

That settled it. When Mrs. Barrett had gone back to her kitchen Alan poured Lucy a glass of sherry.

'This is the first time in weeks that I've had a guest to the house,' he said. 'The last time was when Dr. Wadsworth and his wife came for drinks one Sunday lunch time. A man without a wife tends to neglect the social

138

graces.'

His eyes rested just for a moment on a large silver-framed photograph which stood on top of a bookcase.

The picture was of a laughing young woman with dark hair and sparkling eyes. She was holding on to the mast of a small yacht. Behind was the open sea.

'I was a keen yachtsman at one time,' Alan said, then quietly: 'But all that finished when my wife died. Since then I've been much too busy for such hobbies as sailing.'

She longed to say some words that would comfort him, but they would not come. In any case, she had not known his wife. Mayn't he think it impertinent if she showed too much sympathy with him in his loss? He might look upon it as an intrusion of his grief.

They talked quietly together, about the accident, about their work at the mill. Lucy mentioned her concern that the equipment in her department was so out of date.

'Hardly any of the instruments have been replaced for years,' she said. 'Mr. Earnshaw came down one day and I spoke to him but all he would say was that if Nurse Bailey could manage with what equipment there was, so should I!'

He laughed at her indignation, then apologised.

'I'm sorry! You're quite right, of course. But that's Matthew Earnshaw's attitude through and through. I'll have a word with him. I don't think he'll put me off!'

Later they ate a simple but well-cooked meal in the big dining room across the hall. This was full of heavy dark furniture and must have served old Dr. Bancroft for many years before Alan had come on the scene.

Margy ate with her father and Lucy. She was a little chatterbox and told Lucy about school.

'I like drawing best and reading worst,' she said. 'And I simply hate adding up.'

'You won't get very far if you have to rely on drawing to get you through life,' her father said.

'Do you like listening when someone reads you a story?' Lucy asked.

Margy's little face lit up.

'Ooh, yes, I love it when daddy reads to me before I go to bed at night,' she cried.

'Then if you ever had a little girl of your own wouldn't you like to be able to read to her?'

Margy considered this, then she nodded.

'Yes, I think I would!'

'Then you'll have to learn to read yourself, won't you?'

'And I'd like to teach her sums, I suppose. Yes! I'd like to read to her and teach her sums.'

Lucy met Alan's eyes. He was smiling, a smile that, for some reason, made her heart beat quicker. She looked quickly away and concentrated on Mrs. Barrett's excellent cream trifle.

Later when Alan ran her home he said:

'Margy needs someone like you at her age. I hope you'll come and see us again. And fairly soon.'

'I'd like to,' she murmured.

He said nothing more for a few seconds, then in a low voice he said:

'Thanks—Lucy! I'll always be grateful to you for coming back to Lenthwaite.'


## CHAPTER TWELVE

Rosalind looked up at Mike with shining eyes when, on the following morning, he reported to her in her office.

'It's very decent of you to help me out like this, Mike,' she said. 'When your father told me you'd volunteered to come to manage things for me, I could hardly believe my ears.'

He thought: 'Trust the Old Man to tell a tale like that! Suppose I told her the last thing I want to do is run her mill for her! Volunteered, indeed!'

But he forced a smile and said:

'I'll do the best I can for a few days, Ros. I suppose you'll be looking for someone to take

141

Taylor's place.'

'Yes, of course!' She stood up and went round the desk to his side. 'I'd better show you round and introduce you to the various people you'll be working with.'

As they went from department to department, and toured the long weaving sheds, it seemed strange to Mike that, although he had been born and brought up almost within sight of the Murgatroyd business, he had never been inside the mill before.

His father and Mr. Murgatroyd had always been bitter rivals. When one man secured a profitable contract the other had been passionately angry. Year after year the two had conducted a price cutting war, and their rivalry had become almost a legend in the trade.

Yet it had always been Mr. Earnshaw's ambition, as both Rosalind and Mike knew, that the two of them would marry and bring the two businesses together, under the Earnshaw flag!

Under the Earnshaw flag. There's the rub, Mike mused, as he strode by Rosalind's side through her little empire.

If his father had been reasonable, Mike thought, Mr. Murgatroyd would probably have considered a merger of the two businesses. For it would have been of benefit to both.

'But Dad's not like that,' Mike thought. 'It would be all or nothing. I suppose he long ago decided, even if he got the Murgatroyd business, that he'd never be able to work with its owner. Now he considers the fight is almost over. In his eyes Rosalind doesn't count—except as a wife for me!'

He thought of Lucy. If only she had agreed to marry him and go to London right away, he could have defied his father. But while he was waiting for her to make her mind up, he might as well be useful and help Ros, of whom he was very fond.

'You'd better take over my office,' she said as, their tour completed, they turned back to the administrative block.

'I don't suppose I'll be in the office much of the time,' he said.

She laughed. 'I thought that after daddy died. I soon realised how much paper work there was to do. Of course, I'll help you all I can.'

'I know you will, Ros,' he smiled. 'But I'm here to help *you* so you mustn't spend too much time in the mill.'

She said nothing to that, but her heart was sad. If only she could tell him that all she ever wanted was to be with him, either inside the mill or outside it; but she couldn't. He looked on her only as a sister who was in need of his help. Nothing more...

Mike, to his astonishment, found in the

143

next few days that he actually enjoyed managing the Murgatroyd mill.

He soon realised that, if his father had given him more responsibility, he might have enjoyed helping to manage the Earnshaw's mill just as much. But his father had held him back, smacked him down when he had made suggestions, had laughed scornfully when he had wanted to 'go on the road' and sell Earnshaw cloth.

He had been given humble jobs and had soon grown bored, not only with the Earnshaw mill but with Lenthwaite itself.

Now he found he liked arriving in the mill office at half-past eight in the morning, and, after making a tour of the departments, returning to his own domain to make decisions and tackle the various problems that arise daily in every large business.

Rosalind usually looked in on him about ten o'clock. Often enough he would be discussing something with one of the department heads, and she would give him a smile and, slipping away, return later when he was alone.

'Everything seems to be running very smoothly,' she said, a few days after he had taken up his new job.

'You've got a good workforce, Ros,' he said. 'All they need is a little encouragement from time to time.'

'They all like you, Mike,' she said. 'One of

the weavers said to me yesterday afternoon: "That's a grand young chap, Miss Murtgatroyd. Is he going to stay?"'

He laughed. 'I hope you told her I'm only here till you get another manager.'

'Yes I did! She seemed quite disappointed!'

He thought of the telephone call he had had on the previous evening soon after he reached home. It had come from the agency in London and the petulant voice at the other end of the line had asked why he hadn't done anything about the job he had been offered.

'They won't wait for ever, Mr. Earnshaw,' the agent had said sharply. 'Not even though you do own a helicopter!'

'I can't do anything about it at the moment, Mr. Dell,' Mike had said and briefly explained the position.

'I can give you to the end of the week!' The receiver had been replaced rather sharply at the other end.

Each evening Mr. Earnshaw questioned Mike closely about his day at Murgatroyd's. Often he grumbled because Mike answered shortly and without giving any details.

'Darn it, Mike, this is the chance I've been waiting for!' he exploded once when Mike had refused to answer a question.

'I'm not prepared to give Murgatroyd secrets away just because you've managed to "plant" me in Ros's mill!' Mike snapped and turned away.

He quite enjoyed annoying his father in this way. It served the Old Man right, he thought gleefully. He believed he had placed a spy in the enemy's camp, and now he realises I'm more loyal to Ros than I am to him, my own father.

He found himself admiring Rosalind more and more as the days went by. She had a real grasp of the business side of the mill. Once he complimented her on spotting a flaw in some cloth before it had left for the customer's warehouse.

She had coloured with pleasure at his praise.

'I learnt a lot from my father,' she said. 'Of course, I disappointed him by being a girl when he wanted a son; but when I was quite small he tried to make up for things by teaching me all he knew.'

'I don't see why you want a manager,' he laughed. 'You're quite capable of running the mill on your own.'

But she shook her head.

'The workpeople take more notice of a man,' she said. 'To some of the older hands I'm just a slip of a girl, and however much I know it doesn't make any difference to them.'

Thinking of Lucy he said:

'You don't have a full-time nurse on the premises here at Murgatroyd's?'

She shrugged slim shoulders.

'Dad didn't think it was necessary. He had

two of the overlookers trained in First Aid and they seem able to cope pretty well. In any case, Murgatroyd's isn't as big a firm as Earnshaw's.'

She added: 'By the way, how is Nurse Hirst doing at Earnshaw's? You're quite friendly with her, aren't you, Mike?'

He felt the colour come into his face. He frowned. How much did Ros suspect of his feelings for Lucy?

'She's a nice girl,' he said in a non-committal tone and changed the subject abruptly by mentioning some cloth which was due to leave for a customer in Bradford that afternoon.

Rosalind sighed as she left the office a few minutes later. Mike was in love with Lucy Hirst. There was no doubt in her mind.

'I only hope she makes him happy,' she thought, then fiercely: 'I'll never forgive her if she doesn't.'

Later she went shopping in the town. After she had made one or two purchases at the chemist's she booked an appointment for the following day with her hairdresser.

As she came out into the street again she almost bumped into Dick Hirst. They had known each other since schooldays. He snatched off his hat on seeing her.

'Hullo, Miss Murgatroyd!'

She smiled. 'Why so formal, Mr. Hirst. Not very long ago it was "Ros" and "Dick".'

147

'Before you went away to that posh school near Harrogate,' he reminded her.

'How's work?' she asked. 'You're still a designer at Earnshaw's, aren't you?'

He frowned. 'I suppose so!'

'You don't seem very sure!'

He bit his lip. Suddenly he took her arm. 'Have a cup of tea with me, Ros,' he said, and though she had planned to go back to the mill before it closed, she realised that he was troubled and agreed at once.

They went into Ann's Pantry and Dick ordered tea and cakes.

'I had a row with Mr. Earnshaw this morning,' he said when the waitress had gone away. 'I'd been working on a design for a new sports cloth for quite some time. Today I showed it to him. Do you know what he said?'

She shook her head. His eyes flashed.

'He said he employed me as a designer, not a crossword puzzle compiler!' he cried in disgust.

She wanted to laugh but knew he would be offended if she did.

'Why did he say that?' she asked.

'Because my design incorporated a fairly bold check. Oh, I know all Earnshaw cloths are famous for their conservative patterns, but—well, I think there's room for launching out in another direction from time to time. Why, Earnshaw's hardly ever attempt to cater for the younger end of the market.'

'Never mind, Dick, you can try something else,' she said soothingly.

'If I do it may not be for Earnshaw's,' he said angrily. 'I told Mr. Earnshaw this morning if he wasn't satisfied with my work he knew what to do!'

'Oh, Dick!'

'He called me a cheeky young whippersnapper,' he said indignantly. 'Said I'd better take a day or two off and think things over. So I stormed out.'

'What will you do?' she asked.

She wondered if already he was regretting his loss of temper. Wasn't his indignation a defence mechanism he was using to hide his real fears: that if he wanted to keep his job he would have to apologise humbly to his employer, or that in any case he might lose his position at Earnshaw's, that an apology might not be enough?

'I wish I could get something else,' he said. 'I've not been happy at Earnshaw's for quite a while now. I don't suppose there's anything at your place, Ros?'

Suddenly she thought of Mike. He had only taken the vacant post of manager to help her out in a difficult situation. He had hinted pretty strongly that as soon as she could release him he would be delighted.

Why shouldn't Dick take his place? He might not be as good at the job as Mike, but she would be there to help him through until he became thoroughly accustomed to the work.

And that would let Mike go back to his father's firm where he would be in closer touch with the girl he loved, Dick's sister!

'There's nothing in our design department, Dick,' she said, 'But there might be something else. The only thing is it might upset Mr. Earnshaw more than he's upset already.'

'I don't mind about that! Why should I? He did not mince his words this morning. To hear him talking you'd think he'd wasted his time employing me ever since I went to Earnshaw's mill!'

She drew a deep breath.

'You know that Mike Earnshaw is managing things for me at the moment?'

He nodded. Mike's new job was well known throughout the town.

'How would you like to come and take over, Dick?' she asked. 'I know Mike only took the job on till I could find someone else. It was a purely temporary arrangement. Now—well, in you I may have found the man I'm looking for.'

His face lit up. 'You really mean it?'

She nodded. 'Of course I mean it. I know you haven't had any management experience, but I have and I'll do all I can to help you. You're a sensible man and you know the textile business well enough. What do you say?'

He lifted his cup with a shaking hand and sipped the hot tea before replying, then with a sound that was half-way between a laugh and a sob he said:

'I'll start the minute you say the word, Ros. And thank you! You're a real friend in need.'

Mike was not in his office when Rosalind got back to the mill. She found him discussing an over-due account with the firm's secretary.

'Do you want me?' he asked, looking round and seeing her slender figure in the doorway.

'Yes! I'll wait for you in your office.'

She turned and disappeared. After a couple of minutes he followed.

What a pretty girl Ros was, he thought as he hurried along the dark passages in her wake with the thunder of the looms all about him.

She'd make some lucky man a marvellous wife! If only he hadn't been in love with Lucy, he himself might have—

He told himself not to be a fool as he reached the door of the office he had occupied for just over a week.

Rosalind was standing with her back to the desk. She smiled as he entered.

'Well, I think I've found a new manager,' she said.

He looked at her, startled. He had never

151

expected anything like this.

'But—who is he? Are you sure he's the right man?'

'He's a local man. We both know him well. And he's completely trustworthy.'

'He sounds a paragon. Who is he?'

'Nurse Hirst's brother, Dick,' she said quietly, and as his mouth fell open in amazement: 'I met him in town just now. Apparently he's had a row with your father.'

'But everybody's always having rows with my father,' he cried. 'That means nothing.'

'Apparently it does to Dick Hirst,' she said. 'When I offered him the job as manager he jumped at it. Evidently he had not enjoyed working at Earnshaw's for quite some time.'

'But he's a designer, not a manager, Ros!'

'He's intelligent and has plenty of common sense, and I'll be working with him at first.'

'He may be some of those things, Ros, but I still can't see him running a business like Murgatroyd's.'

She frowned. 'But I thought you only wanted to help me out temporarily, Mike. This is your chance to get out of any obligation you may feel you owe to me.'

He bit his lip. She was right. He had taken the job of manager on very reluctantly. He should be highly delighted that everything had ended so well.

'I don't know what my father will think,' he muttered.

'You'd better go and tell him,' she said, and turned to take some papers up from the desk. Suddenly her eyes had filled with tears and she did not want him to see them.

The hooter signalled the end of the day. Mike looked at the girl standing at the desk, her back to him.

'I'd better be off, then,' he said awkwardly.

She blinked the tears away and looked round at him.

'Thank you for all you've done for me, Mike,' she said. 'I'll always be grateful to you.'

He seemed about to say something, then as if the words would not come, he swung on his heel and hurried from the room.

She went and sat in the chair behind the desk. Only after she had been sitting there, lonelier than she had ever felt before, did it occur to her that Mike had not cleared the drawers of his few possessions.

'I'll send them over to him tomorrow,' she thought. 'I don't suppose he'll come back for them. He's gone out of my life for good now.'

# PART FOUR

# VIOLENCE

## CHAPTER THIRTEEN

'Mr. Earnshaw ought to see a deputation from the workpeople, and that's the truth!' Mr. Hirst exclaimed, a worried expression on his face. 'But he says there's no point in having a meeting when he has no intention of either paying higher wages or allowing his workers to join a union.'

'He seems to be living in the past,' Lucy said, slicing the tender steak on her plate.

'There'll be trouble if he keeps up his present attitude,' her father said unhappily. 'Clem Barraclough and one or two other hot-heads are ripe for a fight.'

'Why don't you have a word with Mr. Earnshaw, Dad?' Mrs. Hirst asked. 'You're one of his oldest employees. He'd probably listen to you.'

'I don't think the time has come for me to interfere,' Mr. Hirst replied. 'If I get involved at this stage there'll be no one who can act as a go-between if things get really difficult.'

The door opened and Dick came into the kitchen. His eyes were dancing with excitement.

'Guess what!' he cried. 'I'm to be manager at Murgatroyd's!'

'You're to be—what?' His father stared at him, unable to believe his ears.

Quickly Dick told of his meeting with Rosalind Murgatroyd and of her offer.

'But what about your job at Earnshaw's?' Lucy asked.

'I shan't be sorry to give that up,' he laughed and told of his brush with his employer which had ended with him walking out earlier that day.

'But you know nowt about management, lad,' Mr. Hirst said, shaking his head.

'Don't forget I went to Earnshaw's when I was sixteen and worked my way up through all the departments until I became a designer. I know quite a bit about the textile trade, as well you know, Dad. Besides, Ros—Miss Murgatroyd—has said she'll help me all she can.'

'And what about Mr. Mike Earnshaw?' his mother wanted to know. 'He was managing Murgatroyd's very well from all accounts.'

'Oh, Mike only took the job on until Ros could get someone to take his place. Well, she's got someone—me!'

Lucy went to the oven and brought his plate of steak and chips to the table. He grinned as he picked up his knife and fork.

'I'm certainly hungry! Being made manager

has given me a rare appetite.'

His father pushed his chair back, and, without a word, made for the back door and his beloved pigeons.

'He's not too pleased, lad,' Mrs. Hirst sighed. 'He was real proud when you were promoted to the Design Department at Earnshaw's.'

'I don't see why he can't be just as proud now I'm to manage Murgatroyd's Mill,' Dick grumbled, scowling at his plate. 'Some folks are never satisfied.'

★　　★　　★

The following day Lucy's first patient was a stout woman who had slipped in the mill yard and twisted her ankle. As Lucy applied a cold water bandage the woman said:

'There's going to be a meeting at dinner time, Nurse.'

'A meeting! What sort of meeting?' Lucy asked.

'Why, everybody's going to protest because Mr. Earnshaw won't see us to discuss our wages. We've gone on long enough letting him have his own way. The time has come for him to meet our demands.'

Lucy frowned. The woman was talking like a parrot. She had obviously been listening to the agitators, who, in the last few days, must have been moving about the mill rousing the passion of the workpeople.

'Won't there be trouble if Mr. Earnshaw hears about your meeting?' she asked.

'There'll be trouble this time whether he hears or not! Either Mr. Earnshaw listens to us—or we go on strike. That's what Clem Barraclough says!'

Lucy sighed as the woman hobbled away. If only there was some way of stopping this meeting which could only lead to trouble. Mr. Earnshaw was a stubborn man. A meeting in the mill yard would only anger him, might even lead to some of the ring-leaders being sacked.

Then what would happen? Would there really be a strike or would the other workers, afraid for their jobs, go quietly back to their looms and carry on? Lucy knew which was most likely.

Yorkshire folk were proud. Even if it meant privation they would stand by their own and defy a man they thought was treating them unfairly.

Half-way through the morning, as Lucy was making herself a cup of coffee, there came a tap on the door of her office and Mike put his head into the room.

'May I come in?' he asked.

'Of course! I'm just making some coffee! Would you like a cup?'

'Sure!' He seated himself beside her desk. 'I suppose you've heard Rosalind

Murgatroyd's given me the sack?'

'Dick told us he'd been appointed her manager when he came in yesterday evening.'

He took the cup she held out to him. As he stirred the coffee he said:

'I hope he's up to the job! Managing a mill isn't quite the same thing as working in a Design Department.'

'Oh, I've no doubt he'll do pretty well. After all, Miss Murgatroyd will help him all she can.'

'I suppose she will! At any rate it's relieved me from having to help her out. That was my father's idea!'

'I heard you did very well. In a way, Miss Murgatroyd will be sorry to see you go, Mike.'

He shrugged. 'I would have stayed if she'd needed me. Now—well, I'm free for other things. And you know what I mean by that, Lucy!'

She did know. He was still hoping she'd say she was willing to go south with him to his new job.

She changed the subject abruptly.

'Have you heard there's to be a meeting in the mill yard at mid-day, Mike?'

He frowned. 'No! No one's told me.'

'The workpeople want more money and your father refuses to see a deputation to discuss the matter.'

He put his cup down on the desk and

jumped up.

'What a fool he is! I knew this would come. He seems to think he's still living in the last century when the mill master was king and whatever he said was law. I'd better go and talk to him.'

She was relieved when he went away. She did not love him. She was sure of that now. But she did not feel like resisting his advances this morning. She had too many other things on her mind.

At twelve o'clock she stood at a window in a passage that looked over the mill yard. Already a sizeable crowd had assembled and she saw a man she recognised as Clem Barraclough, one of the overlookers, carrying a box to a point near the gate. He obviously intended to stand on this and address his fellow workers.

The hooter had already gone for the mid-day break, and more and more men and women poured into the cobbled yard.

Clem Barraclough stood on his box and a cheer went up from the crowd. A tall man in a dark suit standing nearby said something to Clem who nodded as if in agreement.

Lucy wondered who the man was. She didn't recognise him as one of the Earnshaw workpeople.

Presently Clem raised his hand and the hubbub caused by the crowd died away. The window was partly open and the sound of the man's voice reached Lucy.

'You all know why we're here this morning,' the overlooker cried. 'We've been very patient with the management at Earnshaw's. But with the rise in the cost of living, and the fact that we've not had an increase in wages for a long time, the time has come to look after our interests.'

A cheer went up from the crowd. Clem raised his hand again.

'I've made two attempts to persuade Mr. Earnshaw to receive a deputation and talk over this question of wages, but he has turned me down flat each time. We are reasonable people but a time arrives when the patience of even reasonable people becomes exhausted. That is why we are holding this meeting today.'

'If he won't pay up he must do without our labour,' a voice called from the back of the crowd.

A cheer went up. Evidently most of those present agreed with this sentiment.

But Clem Barraclough shook his head. Once again he raised his hand for silence.

'It hasn't come to that yet, lads and lassies,' he cried. 'I'm hoping that you'll pass a resolution today which will empower me to go to Mr. Earnshaw once again and ask for his co-operation.'

'But you've done that before!' a disgusted voice shouted.

'Not quite like what I propose,' the overlooker replied. 'I shall tell Mr. Earnshaw that if wages are not increased substantially we shall take industrial action.'

'You mean, go on strike?' a woman at the front asked, and there was a scared look on her face as if she realised what this would mean to a body of workpeople who would not have a powerful union behind them.

'Yes, that's about the strength of it, Mary Ann,' Clem replied.

'What about us all joining a union?' someone else asked.

Clem looked at the man standing by his side.

'This is Mr. Mortimer from the Union office in Bradford,' he said. 'He's going to urge us all to be united in our demand for union membership. This will be put to Mr. Earnshaw as well as the demand for higher wages. We might as well kill two birds with one stone.'

He stepped down and the union official moved as if to take his place. But before he could mount the box he was pushed aside. Lucy's heart gave a lurch as she saw the thin figure of her father jump up on the temporary rostrum and raise his hands for silence.

There was a mutter from the crowd. Evidently Sam Hirst's appearance at that stage was not welcome.

'Listen to me, friends,' Mr. Hirst cried.

161

'Before you do anything you may regret later, think again. Mr. Earnshaw is not a man to be rushed into anything. If we talk reasonably with him I'm sure he'll see our point of view. As for this talk of joining a union, he'll never agree to that, at least not yet. Why not leave that for another time and just see if we can't get a little more money now!'

There were one or two murmurs of approval from the crowd; but these were drowned in a sudden shout of anger.

'Get off the box, Sam!' someone yelled from the back of the crowd. 'We don't want mealy-mouthed old men like you telling us what to do.'

'Don't go ahead with this talk of strikes and unions,' Sam begged. 'It can only lead to trouble. Mr. Earnshaw's the kind of man who'll bring in labour from outside if you try to force his hand. And that could mean a lot of unemployment—'

He got no further. From the back of the crowd someone threw a stone. It hit the speaker on the forehead and, with a groan, he pitched forward off the box on to the cobbles below.

'Dad!' Lucy sobbed and, turning, ran along the passage to the door that led into the yard outside.

She pushed her way through the now silent crowd, most of whom were appalled by what had happened. Every one of those present had known her father for years. He had been respected and looked up to by all.

She found her father lying, blood oozing from the cut in his forehead, supported by Clem Barraclough. The overlooker glanced up at Lucy. There were tears in his eyes.

'Why had he to interfere?' he asked in despair. 'I told him he'd best keep out of it, for he'd said earlier he didn't agree with what we were doing.'

'You'd better get him into the mill,' Lucy said briskly.

This was no time for recriminations. Her father was injured. She must do the best she could for him.

Willing hands lifted Mr. Hirst, who was now looking round in a bewildered way, and bore him across the yard to the mill door. As they reached it Mr. Earnshaw appeared with Mike.

'What's going on here?' the mill master demanded; then recognising the injured man: 'Why, it's Sam Hirst!'

His face flushed with anger. He turned to the silent crowd and shook his fist at them.

'Now see what your wickedness has done! I'll have the law on you all for this! You ought to be ashamed of yourselves. You—you—'

Words failed him. His face grew purple with passion. Mike put out a hand and touched his arm.

'Dad, take it easy!' he begged. 'You know

very well the doctor told you to take things quietly. You're upsetting yourself.'

'I won't have such goings-on in my own mill yard,' Mr. Earnshaw cried in a strangled voice. 'It isn't right! I'm the head of Earnshaw's. No one else. You—you!—'

He glared around him like a maddened bull, then suddenly putting his hand to his chest, as if stricken by pain, sank slowly to the floor.

Lucy looked at Clem Barraclough.

'Take my father to the First Aid department!' Then looking at Mike who was staring helplessly down at his father's crumpled form: 'Go and ring for an ambulance, Mike.'

'But—' He stared at her helplessly as if too shocked to take in what had happened.

'I think he's had a heart attack,' she said. 'He's best left where he is. I'll stay with him. Don't delay!'

He hurried off and Lucy knelt by the stricken man. She longed to go to her father, but she did not think he needed her as much as Mr. Earnshaw.

The workpeople gathered round, sober and unhappy now, as they gazed down at their employer. One or two of the older women were crying openly, dabbing at their eyes with the corners of their shawls.

The union official came to Lucy's side. His gaunt face was uneasy.

'How bad is he?' he asked.

He was wishing he had not got involved in this business. He had warned Clem Barraclough that it would be no easy task to make Matthew Earnshaw see sense about the union. Now look what had happened.

Lucy did not reply at first then, feeling Mr. Earnshaw's pulse, she said in a low voice.

'He's very ill, very ill indeed.'

Mercifully the ambulance was there in a matter of minutes, and Mr. Earnshaw was rushed off to the local hospital, Mike accompanying him.

Lucy went to her own department to find her father, white and shaken, sitting on a chair and trying to persuade those around him there was nothing much wrong with him.

'How do you feel?' she asked.

'Not so bad,' he said; then anxiously: 'How's Mr. Earnshaw?'

'He's gone to the hospital in the ambulance,' she replied. 'And now let me look at that cut.'

As she washed the wound and put plaster over it the men quietly went from the room. All but Clem Barraclough.

'I'm right sorry this has happened, Sam,' he muttered.

Mr. Hirst smiled sadly.

'These things get out of hand so easily, Clem,' he said. 'But perhaps good will come out of it in the end. Who can tell?'

# CHAPTER FOURTEEN

Mike, leaving the hospital, saw Rosalind walking towards him. She held out her hand to him. Her face was anxious.

'As soon as I heard I had Rawlings bring me here in the mill car,' she said. 'How is your father, Mike?'

He shrugged. His face looked white and careworn.

'It's too early to say, Ros,' he said in a low voice. 'The doctors say he's had a heart attack. They seem to think he'll recover from it with care.'

'It was a dreadful thing to happen. I should think your workpeople must be feeling thoroughly ashamed of themselves!' Ros said indignantly.

He frowned. 'I don't think they're entirely to blame. If dad had seen a deputation and talked things over in a quiet and business-like way, none of this need have occurred. But he refused to listen, then when a meeting was called, he lost his temper and—well, you know what happened.'

'What will you do now, Mike?'

'I shall take over. As far as I can see, dad will be out of action for a very long time. In fact, one of the doctors hinted that, even if he gets well, he'll have to retire from the mill.'

'Poor Mr. Earnshaw,' Rosalind murmured. 'The mill was his whole life, just as it was my father's.'

He smiled faintly.

'I'm going to be glad I spent that time helping you out, Ros,' he said. 'At least I managed to get the rudiments of mill management at Murgatroyd's. It's going to prove very useful in the next few weeks.'

He hesitated then asked:

'How's Dick Hirst shaping up, Ros?'

'I think he'll do the job very well in time. He's a bit strange to it but he's hardly had time to prove himself yet!'

They walked back to the big car waiting outside the hospital gates.

'Can I give you a lift, Mike?' she asked.

'Thanks! I haven't got my car with me. I came to the hospital in the ambulance with dad.'

He sat in the back with Ros and Rawlings, the chauffeur, drove them into Lenthwaite.

'Shall I ask Rawlings to take you home?' Ros asked.

But he shook his head.

'No, I'm going to see Sam Hirst. He was knocked out by a stone when he was talking to the crowd at the mill. I'd like to hear how he is.'

Ros leaned forward and gave the necessary instructions.

'I should think Mr. Hirst's daughter would

be useful when your father had his attack,' she said.

His eyes glowed.

'She was wonderful! She took complete charge. She would have gone to hospital with dad only her own father needed attention. When the ambulance had left the mill she went to treat Mr. Hirst.'

She turned to glance out of the window. One look into Mike's shining eyes had told her how he felt towards Lucy Hirst. Her heart sank. There was no chance of Mike ever looking at her like that.

The big car stopped at the end of Lucy's street. After thanking Rosalind for the lift, he strode away. She watched him halt outside a door and raise his hand to knock. Leaning forward she spoke to the chauffeur.

'Take me home, Rawlings,' she said, then sat back, hands clenched, blue eyes staring miserably before her.

Lucy answered the door to Mike's knock.

'Why, Mike!' she exclaimed in surprise.

'I came to see how your father is,' he said.

'I persuaded him to go to bed and rest,' she said. 'But come in! I'm sure he'll be glad to see you.'

As he followed her up the narrow stairs she asked:

'How's Mr. Earnshaw?'

'The doctors say he should recover. He's in the Intensive Care Unit.'

'It was a terrible thing to happen!'

No more was said and presently Lucy opened a door on the landing above.

'You've got a visitor, Dad,' she said and stood aside so that Mike could go into the bedroom.

Mr. Hirst was sitting propped up against pillows in the big double bed. He was wearing spectacles, but he took these off seeing his employer's son.

'Why, Mr. Mike, I never expected to see you!' he cried.

'I wanted to hear how you were, Mr. Hirst,' Mike said, going forward and sitting on the chair beside the bed.

'Oh, I'll be up tomorrow, never fear,' Mr. Hirst said with a glance at his daughter. 'I wouldn't be lazing in bed now if Lucy hadn't insisted.'

'I'm sure she was right to make you rest,' Mike said. 'You had a nasty shock apart from any injury the stone caused.'

Mr. Hirst wanted to know about Mr. Earnshaw's condition and Mike told him the little there was to tell. The older man listened in silence then asked:

'I suppose you'll carry on, Mr. Mike?'

'I shall do my best.'

Mr. Hirst hesitated then said:

'May I make a suggestion to you?'

'I wish you would, Mr. Hirst. I need all the advice I can get just now, especially from people of common sense like you.'

Lucy standing by the door smiled to herself. This was a new Mike Earnshaw. Gone was the brash headstrong young man whose only ambition had been to spread his wings and leave Lenthwaite as far behind as possible.

Now, in an emergency, his real character was showing through. Dreadful though the events leading up to his father's heart attack had been, they had at least brought Mike to his senses and shown him the path he must take.

'I think the time has come to take the workfolk at Earnshaw's more into the management's confidence, Mr. Mike,' Sam Hirst said slowly. 'You'll be in charge now. Couldn't you meet Clem Barraclough and the others half-way and talk things over with them?'

Mike frowned at the carpet.

'If I did anything like that, and word of it reached my father, it could kill him,' he muttered.

'It needn't get to his ears, lad,' Sam said. 'You could see that any talks you had with Clem were in private. I don't say you should meet any demands that are made about higher wages and the workers joining a union, but you could talk things over quietly and soberly and see what plans could be made for the future. Then when your father was feeling

better you could act as spokesman. He'd
listen to you where he'd never listen to Clem
or the union official.'

Mike nodded. 'I'll see Barraclough
tomorrow. He seems a sensible sort of chap.
We should be able to iron something out
between us that will give promise for the
future.'

'Good lad!' the older man said approvingly.
'There's nothing like bringing things out into
the open for clearing the air.'

Mike stayed a few minutes more then,
accompanied by Lucy, he went downstairs.
Mrs. Hirst was sitting before the fire in the
kitchen and he answered her questions about
his father then said he must be going.

'I left mother at the hospital,' he said. 'I'm
going to pick my car up at the mill then I'll go
back for her.'

'Poor lady, she'll be very upset,' Mrs. Hirst
said.

'Yes, it was quite a shock!' he agreed; then
saying goodnight he went out into the narrow
hall with Lucy.

In the half light he looked down into her
face.

'Lucy, what about—us?' he asked in a low
voice.

She shook her head.

'Oh, Mike, this isn't the time to talk about
that now.'

He nodded. 'I suppose not. At any rate,

171

there'll be no question of my going away from Lenthwaite, at least not for some time to come. But I shan't give up, Lucy. I'll see you every day from now on so sooner or later you'll have to make up your mind about me.'

Then he was gone and she was left to close the door and stand in the dark little hall for a few moments, eyes closed, thinking of another man who, not very long ago, had said: 'I'll always be grateful to you for coming back to Lenthwaite.'

With a sigh she made for the kitchen again. Her mother looked up.

'That young man's in love with you, Lucy,' she said. 'It's a pity you can't feel the same way towards him.'

Lucy picked up some sewing she had put down when she had gone to answer Mike's knock.

'Life isn't like that, Mum,' she murmured. 'The things we want are usually well out of reach. Others lose their appeal because they're always there to be picked up whenever we feel like it.'

'And I suppose that's how you feel about Mike Earnshaw?'

Lucy nodded. 'You can't love to order, Mum. I sometimes wish one could.'

She got up. She didn't want to talk any more about Mike with her mother.

'I'll just go up and see if dad wants anything,' she said and made for the door.

Mrs. Hirst sighed as she stared into the fire. What a wonderful thing it would have been if Lucy had married Mike Earnshaw!

But that wasn't to be. She knew enough about her daughter to know when she had made up her mind about something.

In the morning Mike, seated in his father's office, told Bessie Shaw to send for Clem Barraclough.

As he waited he thought of the conversation he had had with the doctor at the hospital earlier that morning.

His father, he had been told, was holding his own.

'In fact I'm more hopeful today than I was when he came in yesterday,' the doctor had said.

'You think he'll get better?'

'It's early days to be sure, Mr. Earnshaw, but my view is that he'll get over this attack, though he'll have to lead a very quiet life for a long time to come. No business worries, for instance.'

'I think I can promise he'll have none of those,' Mike said.

'He's lucky to have a son who can step into his shoes,' the other had said and, after promising to telephone if there was any sudden change in Mr. Earnshaw's condition, the doctor rang off.

Mike listened to the comforting hum of the looms at work which filled the air.

To his relief all the workpeople had returned that morning. There had been no further talk of a strike.

From what Bessie had told him Mr. Earnshaw's heart attack had acted like a shower of cold water on the hot-heads who had been calling for strike action.

'They're ashamed of themselves, Mr. Mike,' she said. 'When someone threw that stone at Mr. Hirst they began to regret what had happened; then when they saw your father taken off in the ambulance, the whole thing collapsed. I don't think there'll be any strike now.'

There came a tap at the door. Bessie Shaw appeared.

'Mr. Barraclough's here, Mr. Mike,' she said, then ushered the big overlooker into the office.

'Sit down, Clem,' Mike said, indicating the chair set before the desk.

Clem sat down a little apprehensively. When Mike had sent for him he had wondered if it would be to give him his cards and tell him he was sacked.

He had slept little on the previous night. He had been really upset by Mr. Earnshaw's heart attack. He knew that if he had not called the meeting in the mill yard on the previous day Mr. Earnshaw would very likely have been as hale and hearty as ever.

Mike looked at the burly figure in the long

grey overall coat the mill overlookers wore. He had known Clem since he was a little boy. It had been Clem who had walked round the mill with him when, out of curiosity, he had ventured into the noisy weaving sheds.

'Well, Clem!' he said now, and the older man shook his head sadly.

'I'm right sorry for what happened yesterday, Mr. Mike,' he said. 'I hope the news about your father is a little better today.'

'He seems to be holding his own,' Mike replied; then leaning forward, hands clasped on the desk top: 'I wanted to have a talk to you, Clem, about the future.'

Relief flooded Clem Barraclough's heart. So he wasn't to be sacked, after all.

'What had you in mind, Mr. Mike?'

'I want you to know—and I want you to tell the other people who work in the mill—that I sympathise with their views. I'm more progressive than my father in that I think you should have higher rates of pay and be allowed to join a union, if you feel so minded.'

Clem said nothing. It was good to hear that the young gaffer thought as he did, but after all, Mike Earnshaw wasn't in charge yet. He had just taken over temporarily until his father returned.

'Obviously I can't do anything immediately,' Mike went on. 'We'll have to
175

wait and see how my father progresses; but from what I've so far been able to find out at the hospital, my father isn't likely to play a big part in running Earnshaw's in the future.'

'So things will have to go on as before—for the time being?'

'I want you—and the others—to be patient for a while, Clem. I had a talk yesterday evening with Mr. Hartley, the company secretary, and my mother, who's a director of the firm, and they feel as I do, that we can't make a big move yet. Let's see how my father goes on, then when he's well enough for a discussion, the three of us should be able to convince him that several changes should be made.'

'That sounds promising, Mr. Mike. I'll report back to my committee and let them know what you've just told me.'

'You think they'll hold their hand and not talk about having any strike?'

'I think I can influence them. I know that Sam Hirst will back me up.'

Mike stood up and went round the desk. As Clem rose he held out his hand.

'I'm sure we can bring something good out of this whole unhappy affair, Clem,' he said. 'A little patience is all I ask just now. Later I think we'll be talking about higher wages geared to better production.'

'And—the union?'

'There shouldn't be any difficulty about

that. It seems to work well enough at Murgatroyd's, as I found out when I acted as manager for just over a week.'

When Clem had gone Mike rang for Bessie. She came in with her notebook thinking he wanted to dictate letters. But he shook his head.

'I wanted to ask you something, Bessie,' he said. 'How's Dick Hirst shaping up at Murgatroyd's now he's been appointed manager.'

Bessie's pretty face coloured.

'I don't really know, Mr. Mike,' she replied. 'Of course it's early days yet. He's only been there a day or two. Besides—'

'Besides—what?' he asked. 'I thought you and he were—well, sweet on each other.'

She frowned. 'I don't see why you should say that, Mr. Mike. I'm Lucy's best friend and Dick and I grew up together. But—well, as for being sweet on each other—'

'Oh, come on, Bessie,' he laughed. 'Everyone knows you'll get married some day or other.'

Her eyes flashed. His words had made her angry.

'I think Dick might have other plans,' she said sharply. 'After all, Miss Murgatroyd's a very pretty girl and—well, she has made him her manager. She—she—'

'Good God, you don't mean—?' he gasped. 'But Rosalind Murgatroyd would never marry

Dick Hirst. She—she couldn't!'

'I don't see why not,' she said quietly. 'And now, if you don't need me any more, Mr. Mike, I've a lot of work to do outside.'

He said no more and she went back to the outer office. But for several seconds after she had gone he stood there staring at the closed door, a look of consternation on his good-looking face. Ros and Dick Hirst! Why, it was impossible, quite impossible...

## CHAPTER FIFTEEN

'I was sorry not to be there when it happened,' Alan Tolson said. 'But from all reports you handled the situation very well, Lucy. I gather Mr. Earnshaw is progressing favourably.'

He had arrived at the mill at ten o'clock. There were no workpeople to see him and, as he had a heavy visiting list, he told Lucy he would be glad of the extra time to enable him to catch up.

'At least you must stay for a cup of coffee,' she said. 'I'm just going to make one.'

He smiled. 'I'll be glad to. A quarter of an hour won't make much difference. I'll still be able to get through my round by lunch-time.'

'How's Margy?' Lucy asked.

She had been delighted to see him and was

surprised to find she was disappointed he would not be spending the whole morning at the mill.

'Oh, Margy is her usual wilful little self,' he said. 'She asked me last night, as I was tucking her up in bed, when Nursie would be coming to see her again. I said I would issue an invitation when I came to the mill this morning. How about coming to tea next Sunday, Lucy?'

'I'd love to!' she said, handing him his coffee. 'I'll look forward to seeing Margy again.'

His grey eyes twinkled. 'I rather hoped you might have said you were looking forward to seeing me.'

She felt the colour come into her cheeks. She made a great business of pouring her own coffee so he would not see her confusion.

As they sat in the quiet little room Alan told Lucy that her father had suffered no ill effects from the wound caused by the stone.

'I looked in before I came here,' he said. 'You were wise to insist on him staying in bed today, Lucy.'

She laughed. 'I don't think he'll be in bed when I go home at lunch time,' she said. 'I shouldn't be surprised if he doesn't come back to work tomorrow morning.'

He was spared a reply to this by the ringing of the telephone bell. Lucy answered it.

'It's your housekeeper,' she said holding

out the receiver. 'She seems quite upset about something.'

He spoke briefly to the agitated old woman at the other end of the line, then turned to Lucy. His face was white.

'It's Margy,' he said. 'Mrs. Barrett says she's disappeared.'

Lucy frowned. 'Disappeared! But where can she have gone?'

'I don't know but I must start looking for her. She's a venturesome little thing. The sooner I locate her the better.'

He made for the door. Lucy called after him:

'Let me know if you find her—Alan. If you don't I want to help you look for her.'

He glanced back. Just for a moment their eyes met.

'Thank you, Lucy,' he said quietly. 'I know I can rely on you to help in any way possible.'

Then he was gone and she, picking up the coffee cups, carried them to the little sink in the corner. Suddenly, for no reason at all, she felt tremendously happy.

When an hour had passed without any call from Alan, Lucy rang his house. Mrs. Barrett answered. The old woman's voice was tearful.

'She's not turned up,' she said. 'Dr. Tolson has gone to the police for help. They're searching for her now.'

'Has she disappeared before?' Lucy asked.

'Not for as long as this. She once slipped away and I found her in a garden further down the road.'

As Lucy replaced the receiver the door opened and Mike came into the room.

'You look upset,' he said.

'Dr. Tolson's little girl has disappeared,' she replied. 'I was just asking his housekeeper if they had found her. But they haven't.'

'She's probably hiding somewhere. From all accounts she's a mischievous little thing. It's the sort of trick she'd play on her father.'

'But she's been missing for over an hour. Her father has gone to the police.'

He slipped his arm about her slim waist and gave her a little hug.

'Don't take it to heart so, Lucy. After all, an hour isn't a lifetime. She'll turn up, depend upon it.'

She drew away from him.

'Was there something you wanted?' she asked.

He nodded. 'I was remembering how you told me you'd approached my father about re-equipping your department. Now that he's in hospital and not likely to interfere, I'd like you to make a list of everything you feel you need and I'll order it from the medical suppliers.'

'Do you think you should?' She frowned. 'What will your father say when he comes back to the mill and finds what you've done.'

He laughed. 'I don't think he'll be coming back for a very long time, if at all, Lucy! No! You go ahead and make your list. I'll see you get all the equipment you need.'

'How is your father, Mike?' she asked.

He shrugged. 'The doctors say very little. He's getting on as well as can be expected. He's still in the Intensive Care Unit, of course, and likely to stay there for some time.'

'And you're running the mill?'

'For the time being.'

'And the other job—the job you were offered in London?'

'I'm afraid that's off. I can't just walk out now when there's no one else to take Dad's place. Later—if by a miracle the Old Man did take up the reins again—I might think about it again.'

There came a tap at the door. Lucy went to answer it and found two young women outside. One had a white face and was clinging tightly to the other, a girl of about seventeen.

'Please, Miss, Lizzie's having one of her turns,' the girl said. 'I brought her to you.'

'Bring her in here,' Lucy said and led the way to the little Rest Room.

'Does she often have these turns?' Lucy asked.

'Every few weeks. She has some tablets she takes, but she says she left them at home this morning, she was in such a hurry to get to work.'

Lucy told her patient to lie still until she felt better and sent the other girl back to her loom. Only when she was alone with her patient did she realise that Mike must have slipped away a few minutes before.

'When you feel better you'll go home for the rest of the day,' Lucy told the girl; then added severely: 'And let this be a lesson to you. Don't forget your tablets in future.'

'No, Nurse, I won't,' the other promised humbly.

It was only when she was alone again that Lucy remembered about the missing child. Once again she dialled the number of Alan Tolson's house.

Mrs. Barrett told her there was still no news.

'The doctor's still out searching for her,' the old woman said. 'The police are helping him.'

'Why wasn't she at school today?' Lucy asked curiously.

'It's half term. The schools are on holiday.'

When she rang off, Lucy stood undecided. If only she could be with Alan helping to look for Margy.

But her place was here at the mill. She was having the quietest day since she had come to take charge of Earnshaw's First Aid department; but that did not mean that, as soon as she abandoned her post, some emergency might not arise.

When the hooter sounded at mid-day and she heard the thunder of the looms die away, she hurried from the mill. Instead of going home she headed across the town to Alan Tolson's house.

'Any news yet?' she asked the old housekeeper.

Mrs. Barrett dried her eyes with the corner of her apron.

'No, none at all. I haven't seen the doctor for nigh on two hours.'

'She mustn't have been found or you would have heard,' Lucy said. 'Perhaps we could ring the police station. They might know something.'

'Will you do it?' Mrs. Barrett asked. 'I haven't liked to.'

So Lucy rang the police; but all they could tell her was that the search was continuing and that they did not know where Dr. Tolson might be. Turning from the telephone Lucy found Mrs. Barrett sobbing bitterly.

'If only I'd been watching her more closely,' the old woman whimpered. 'But I had my work to do. When I went to look for her—I thought she seemed very quiet—she'd gone.'

'It wasn't your fault,' Lucy comforted.

'But the doctor will blame me if anything happens to her.'

'Nothing is going to happen to her. She'll turn up safe and sound. She's probably with one of the neighbours now.'

But Lucy's heart sank as she spoke. All the neighbours must be aware by this time that Margy had disappeared. The police would have seen to that.

'If only there was something I could do,' she thought. 'But there isn't. I must just sit and wait.'

Alan arrived back at the house just before one o'clock. He looked exhausted. He seemed to have aged ten years since Lucy had seen him earlier that morning.

He seemed glad to see her. She made him sit down and brought him coffee and sandwiches which Mrs. Barrett had prepared a few minutes earlier for herself and Lucy.

A little colour returned to his gaunt face as he ate and drank. Lucy did not worry him with questions until he had eaten. At last he looked at her.

'Shouldn't you be at the mill?' he asked.

She shook her head.

'I rang Mike Earnshaw a few minutes ago and he said he'd ask one of the overlookers to stand in for me this afternoon. He's trained in First Aid and often helped Nurse Bailey.'

'I'm glad. I need to feel a little moral support.'

He then told her what a nightmare the morning had been. The police had mounted a full scale search but no trace of Margy had been found.

'I've simply toured the town looking in back streets and courtyards and alleys.' In despair he added: 'She could be anywhere. She might have fallen and injured herself and not be able to move.'

'She'll be found, I'm sure of it,' Lucy said.

'But you hear such awful things these days about young children being abducted. She might be miles away by now. She's a trusting little soul, and though I've told her over and over again not to talk to strangers, it just isn't in her not to respond to a kindly word. If she was in the street and a man in a car stopped and spoke to her she—she—'

He broke off and buried his face in his hands. Lucy timidly touched his shoulder.

'We must go on searching for her,' she said, and he looked up at her.

'We?'

'I'd like to help. There must be lots of places that haven't been covered yet.'

He stood up. 'You're right, Lucy. I'm a poor chap to give way so easily.'

The telephone shrilled in the hall. Alan ran from the room and reached it before Mrs. Barrett had left the kitchen.

'Yes? The police! Have you some news for me?' Lucy heard him ask eagerly.

He listened and Lucy held her breath. Did this mean that Margy had been found?

186

Alive—or dead?

At last Alan replaced the receiver and turned to her.

'They've found a tiny handkerchief on a track leading up to the moor,' he said dully. 'They described it. It has Donald Ducks embroidered on it. It's certainly Margy's.'

'They think she's gone up on the moor?'

'Yes! They're extending the search now. Pray God they find her before it gets dark. The moor's a big place.'

He made for the front door.

'Where are you going?' Lucy cried.

He frowned as he glanced back.

'On to the moor. I must help in the search.'

'I'll come with you!' Lucy looked towards the kitchen where Mrs. Barrett was standing. 'You take any phone calls, Mrs. Barrett, in case the police ring.'

Then she followed Alan from the house.

They found a police car parked at the bottom of the steep track that led up to the moor. The sergeant sitting at the wheel said he had been left to direct searchers up on to the moor.

'Other police units will be coming from districts around, doctor,' he said. 'At the moment there are few of our own men available. Later this afternoon there'll be enough from outside to extend the search, and then there'll be more chance of finding the child.'

Alan turned and, hardly seeming to notice that Lucy was following him, began to climb the track through the heather.

Lucy's heart was heavy. The moor was a treacherous place, especially for a six-year-old. There were so few landmarks that it was easy for an adult to get lost. A child, once she had lost her bearings, would just wander about the boggy waste until she sank down from exhaustion. And, once she was lying in the heather, the chances of finding her would be reduced almost to nil.

As they reached the top of the track Alan stood and looked up at the sky. Lucy followed the direction of his gaze and her heart sank.

She guessed what he was thinking. The blue skies of earlier that morning had gone to be replaced by dark lowering clouds.

She knew only too well what this meant.

At any moment a mist could come down on the moor which would make the search for the missing child trebly hard, if not impossible.

Alan turned to look at her. There was despair in his face now.

'Pray God they find her before the moor is blotted out,' he muttered, then before she could speak, he swung away and hurried along the faint track once more.

Lucy did not follow for a few moments. An unaccustomed sound had come to her ears.

188

She had heard it once before, on the day after her return to Lenthwaite from London.

Her heart rose. So Mike had joined the search party!

As she stood there she saw the helicopter away to her left. It was flying low over the moor. She thought she could see a figure at the controls through the transparent perspex windshield.

She hurried after Alan. He too had paused hearing the helicopter.

'Surely we'll find her now,' Lucy said, coming to his side.

He looked round. His face was grim.

'Even a helicopter won't be much use when the mist covers the moor,' he said then, hands thrust deep in pockets, shoulders hunched, he went forward, eyes searching the rough heather-covered ground for the fragment of humanity who was everything in the world to him.

## CHAPTER SIXTEEN

A message came through on a police walkie-talkie later that afternoon that another child, a girl aged nine, had been reported missing half an hour before.

Alan and Lucy, walking over the moor at the end of the long police line, looked round

189

as a shout reached them.

It came from a police inspector who, having caught their attention, hurried over the rough ground towards them.

He told them of the message.

'It rather looks as if this older child may have met up with your little girl, doctor,' the inspector said, 'and persuaded her to go up on the moor with her.'

'What's the child's name?'

'Betty Capper!'

'Her mother and father are patients of mine. Once or twice she's come to the house to play with Margy, who is very fond of her,' Alan said.

'She wasn't reported as missing until just now as, apparently her mother believed she was playing with a schoolfriend. It's the half-term holiday. When she didn't turn up at lunch time they made some enquiries, then started searching. I suppose when they found out that little Margy was missing as well, they thought it was time to go to the police.'

Alan looked hopelessly round the moor. The mist was closing in fast and visibility was down to fifty yards or so. The men at the end of the police line were now only vague shapes moving through the thickening haze.

Overhead Lucy could hear the helicopter still searching. She looked up as its dark shape swept above the long line of searchers and disappeared into the low cloud.

'They won't be able to fly much longer,' the inspector said, noticing Lucy's upward glance.

'Isn't Mr. Earnshaw by himself in the helicopter?' she asked in surprise.

'He was at first, but about half an hour ago he went back to pick up Miss Murgatroyd,' the Inspector replied. 'I suppose he decided that two pairs of eyes were better than one, and as she had apparently volunteered he took her aboard. He sent a radio message to me.'

A light drizzle was now falling to add to the discomfort of the searchers.

'Let's go on,' Alan said through clenched teeth, and Lucy, glancing at his tense pale face, knew that he was about at the end of his tether.

They plodded on. Lucy was glad of the coat she was wearing, for though there was little wind, it was cold on the moor. Alan had on a short car coat he usually wore when visiting patients.

Earlier Lucy had questioned Mrs. Barrett about Margy and had heard to her relief that the old woman had insisted on the child wearing an anorak when she had gone out to play, for in spite of the earlier sunshine, it had been a chilly morning for early spring.

'At any rate she'll be reasonably warm,' Lucy thought, then flinched instinctively as the helicopter came back and passed only a few feet above their heads. Its whirling rotor blades drew the coarse moorland grass almost flat against the wet ground.

'They'd better watch it,' the police inspector muttered, 'or we'll be looking for them, as well, if they crash.'

Alan looked at Lucy.

'I'm tired of walking at the end of this long line,' he muttered. 'I've a feeling we'll never find Margy this way. I'm going off on my own. I've a hunch we ought to be searching the other side of the moor.'

'I shouldn't advise it, doctor,' the inspector said sharply. He had overheard Alan's words. 'The only way to find people in these conditions is by methodical progression of a line of searchers going backwards and forwards.'

But Alan shook his head.

'That may be the police way,' he said. 'It's not mine. I'm going to strike out on my own. If we don't find the children soon darkness will fall then they're likely to be out all night.'

He turned and started across the moor walking rapidly away from the police line. Lucy hesitated. She couldn't see him disappear into the mist like this. She must go with him, even if he was acting against police advice.

As she made after him she heard the inspector's voice calling after her. But she took no heed of him. She quickened her pace for already Alan's tall form was but a hazy shadow ahead of her in the thickening mist.

'Alan, wait for me!' she called.

She started to run risking a broken ankle as she plunged through the tussocks of heather and the rivulets which criss-crossed the moor at this point.

She might have caught up with him if a sudden swirl of mist had not hidden him from sight at the very moment that she stumbled into an evil-smelling bog.

She felt the cold water rise to her knees as she turned and struggled back on to firmer ground.

By the time she looked round for Alan again, he had disappeared completely into the mist and she was alone with no sound to break the silence around her.

Even the distant drone of the helicopter's engines had died away...

\*     \*     \*

Mike landed the helicopter in the grounds of his father's house. For several seconds he made no attempt to climb out or speak to the girl by his side.

'There's nothing else you can do, Mike,' Rosalind said. 'The mist is far too thick for you to go on searching from the air.'

He frowned. Opening the door at his side he jumped out then went round the machine to help Rosalind out.

They stood side by side on the landing pad and looked back towards the hill at the back of Lenthwaite which rose to the moor.

The top of the hill was lost in mist. Down here except for a light drizzle visibility was good.

Rosalind shivered. Once or twice as she and Mike had swooped low over the moor her heart had been in her mouth. At any moment she had expected the ungainly machine to hit a sudden rise in the ground and come crashing in ruins to the heather.

Worried though she was by the plight of the lost child, she was glad to be safe on the ground again with Mike by her side.

'I suppose I'm a coward,' she thought, 'but—oh, I was terrified up there. I must admit it.'

A man ran forward. He looked at Mike.

'Shall I take over, sir?' he asked.

But Mike shook his head. His face was set in stern lines.

'No, Barnes! I'm going up again.' He turned to Rosalind. 'I brought you back, Ros, because I didn't think it fair to go on risking your life.'

'But, Mike!' She stared at him in stunned dismay. He couldn't mean that he was returning to the moor, not in these conditions.

'I must go back, Ros,' he said gently. 'I can

cover so much more ground than the others. It could take them days to search the moor properly, and the child could die of exposure if she had to spend a night outside in these conditions.'

'I won't let you go!' she cried and grabbed his arm.

Gently but firmly he released himself from her frenzied grip. He began to climb back into the helicopter's small cabin.

Barnes stepped forward.

'Is it wise to go up again, sir?' he asked. 'The mist is very low. It will make flying difficult if not dangerous.'

But Mike ignored him. He looked at the girl.

'Go up to the house, Ros,' he said. 'My mother will give you some tea. You look very cold.'

'Mike, don't go!' she sobbed. 'I can't bear it. I—I love you.'

The rotors started up with a roar completely drowning her words.

A gust from the whirling blades almost swept Ros off her feet. The man by her side steadied her.

Together they stood watching the helicopter rise from the pad and soar away towards the moor.

When it had passed out of sight Barnes said gently.

'I think you'd better do as Mr. Mike

suggested, miss. Go to the house and have a cup of tea with Mrs. Earnshaw. I believe she's just returned from the hospital.'

Ros forced a smile, thanked him, then, turning, made her way through the drizzle, towards the house in the distance.

Mike, flying low over the moor, saw, through a sudden break in the mist, the long line of policemen plodding purposefully forward as they searched for the missing children.

He turned away from them. They were quite capable of covering that part of the moor, he decided. He would make for the eastern slopes which had so far not been searched.

The mist billowed up at him and he bit his lip in exasperation as he tried to peer through it to the ground below.

It was like flying in soup. Perhaps Barnes had been right to point out that using the helicopter in these conditions was dangerous.

Then suddenly the mist thinned and he could just see the ground again. This time he gave a low whistle. For just ahead of him was a hunched plodding figure.

A pale face was lifted to him and he recognised Dr. Tolson.

He flew on. Alan Tolson would not thank him for landing and suggesting he joined him in the helicopter. Better to carry on independently.

With the doctor covering the ground and the helicopter sweeping backwards and forwards over the moor, there was more chance of finding the lost children than if they worked together.

He reached the far side of the moor and came round in a wide sweep. The mist had closed in again and now it was like flying through cotton wool.

The windscreen wipers went backwards and forwards to clear the drizzle; but they could not thin the mist.

Mike peered down but nothing was to be seen below. It was as if he was suspended half-way between heaven and earth.

He glanced at the altimeter.

'A hundred feet,' he muttered. 'If I go down to fifty feet I might see more. It's risky—but it may be worth it.'

The little machine answered the controls and the nose went forward.

The ground seemed to rush up at him. He saw the darkness of the moor skimming below and he held his breath, his hand on the joystick.

The mist was thinner here and he peered ahead through narrowed eyes.

It was a part of the moor he did not know very well. He wondered if there were any trees, those small thorns which were occasionally to be found growing amongst the heather.

There were no trees.

But there was something else.

A cluster of rocks which, with dramatic suddenness loomed up ahead of the helicopter.

Desperately Mike took evasive action. But he was too late. Though he missed the rocks the helicopter stalled, hung in the air for a couple of seconds, then fell like a wounded bird to the moor below.

# CHAPTER SEVENTEEN

Lucy stood, listening.

At first when she had heard it she had thought the thin shrill cry had been a curlew's as it flew above the mist-enshrouded moor.

But now she was not so sure. The cry could have come from the lips of a child—a frightened, exhausted child.

She looked around trying to penetrate the thick wall of mist. But she could hardly see any further than the tips of her fingers when she extended her hand.

She had been hopelessly lost for at least a quarter of an hour.

She had tried to follow Alan but had soon given up. Alan had vanished into the mist as if he had never existed.

She had completely lost her sense of

direction, and though at first she had called out, hoping someone would hear her cry, the sound had seemed to bounce back from the impenetrable white wall which had closed in on her.

'Hullo!' she shouted. 'Is there someone there?'

She listened and was rewarded by a faint cry. Her heart rose. There was someone quite close by. If she could only pin point the direction from which the call had come she could make off in that direction and join up with whoever it turned out to be.

She called out again. Once more a cry came in reply.

'Keep calling!' she shouted. 'I'll come to you!'

Two voices now sounded. They came from Lucy's right and she made off in that direction.

'I'm coming! I'm coming!' she cried.

The ground underfoot was treacherous. More than once Lucy stumbled over a tussock of heather or a loose stone.

Suddenly a dark shape launched itself at her. A pair of arms went round her knees almost bringing her down.

'There, there! Steady now,' she said and bent over the child, who was clinging to her and sobbing uncontrollably.

'You're going to be all right now, Margy,' she murmured, bending to gather the child to her.

'We was frightened,' the little voice sobbed. 'Betty and me was frightened.'

'Well, you're going to be all right now, love,' Lucy said, kissing the top of the curly head.

She looked round.

'But where is Betty?' she asked.

'I'm here,' another voice said and out of the mist came an older child who stood looking a little uncertainly at her rescuer.

'Can we go home now?' Margy asked.

Lucy bit her lip. What did one reply to a question like this? A child as young as Margy had complete confidence in grown-ups. Now that she had been found she would expect to be taken home immediately.

'I'm afraid we'll have to be patient for a little bit longer,' Lucy said. 'Very soon someone will come along and show us the way home.'

'But don't you know the way?' Betty demanded.

She was a solemn round-faced little girl and she fixed her brown eyes on Lucy in a disillusioned stare.

Lucy was at a loss. The children looked cold—Margy was shivering—and she tried not to think that, if the mist did not lift, they might have to spend the night in the open.

'I tell you what,' she said brightly. 'Let's see how loudly we can shout. First I'll shout then you, Betty, see if you can make as much noise as me. After that, Margy will show us what she can do.'

The two children nodded. This was a game of sorts and welcome after the fears of the last few hours.

So Lucy lifted up her voice in a loud yell. Betty followed and performed very creditably. Even Margy managed to give a good account of herself.

'Again!' Lucy shouted and once more her shout rang out.

But the children soon tired of the game.

'I know what we'll do now,' Lucy said. 'We'll all shout together. Are you ready?'

Once again the three voices rang out, this time in unison.

Lucy listened. She thought she heard a faint shout somewhere across the moor, but, though they shouted again, the reply was not repeated.

It was growing dark now. Lucy looked round in despair.

She must find some kind of shelter if they were to be forced to spend the night on the moor. The children were cold and exhausted. She dreaded to think what a night in the open in these conditions might not do to them.

'We'll start walking,' she said. 'It will help us to get warm.'

'When are we going home?' Margy demanded, slipping her little hand into

Lucy's.

'Very soon now,' Lucy replied. 'I think we could do with a rest first.'

'You don't know the way home, do you?' Betty said accusingly. 'If you did you'd have set off before this.'

Lucy did not reply to this. With Margy's hand in hers she started to make her way over the rough uneven ground praying that a cluster of rocks, some trees, a small hillock, might appear through the mist to give them some sort of shelter.

The children were almost at the end of their strength. Once Betty flopped down in the wet heather and announced that she wasn't going to go another step.

Lucy swung Margy up into her arms. She smiled down at the other child.

'Come along, Betty,' she said encouragingly. 'Perhaps we haven't much further to go. I do believe the mist is thinning a little.'

It wasn't, but her words brought Betty to her feet again and the little party stumbled forward once more.

Then quite unexpectedly a dark mass rose out of the moor a few yards ahead of them.

Lucy's heart rose. What was this? A rock—or something more substantial?

It turned out to be a ruined shepherd's hut. It had no door and only a hole in the thick walls for a window.

But it had a pile of dry heather in one corner and offered a refuge from the drizzle and mist outside.

The two children sank gladly on to the heather while Lucy considered her next move.

If the worst came to the worst they would at least have shelter for the night. In the morning, when the mist lifted, they would surely be found fairly quickly.

'I'm hungry!' Betty said in the background.

'I'm thirsty!' Margy declared.

'Why don't you lie down and try to have a little sleep?' Lucy suggested; but her heart had sunk even further now that food and drink had been mentioned.

Children needed something to eat and drink at regular intervals. It seemed likely that there would be nothing to give them until the searchers found them.

'I can't even go and search for water,' she thought, 'for I've nothing to carry it in even if I find it.'

She went back to the children.

'Now I want you to be very brave little girls,' she said quietly. 'Until someone comes along we must stay here. It is better than being out there in the mist and the rain.'

'I want my mummy,' Betty sobbed.

'I want my daddy,' Margy wailed.

Lucy went back to the doorway and looked out into the half-light. Darkness would come even earlier than usual, thanks to the mist and rain.

Their chances of being found until next day were receding with every moment that passed.

Suddenly in desperation she raised her voice in a piercing shout.

'Help! Help!' she yelled then listened hopefully as the silence closed in on her again.

Then her heart gave a sudden lurch. For she had heard, not an answering cry but the sound of approaching footsteps.

A few seconds later a dark figure loomed out of the mist. She ran towards it.

'Thank God you've come,' she sobbed in relief, recognising Alan. 'I've found the children.'

Strong arms went round her, a face looked into hers.

'Lucy!' the man's voice said. 'Thank God you're all safe.'

Then he put her gently aside and went forward into the darkness of the little hut.

Two hours later, with the children fast asleep, Alan and Lucy sat side by side and talked in low voices.

'Lucky I had that block of chocolate in my pocket,' Alan said. 'I was taking it to young Ted Abson. He had polio as a child and this is his birthday.'

'Lucky too that you were able to find that

stream and take the children to it in turn,'
Lucy added. 'At least they were able to eat
and drink before they went to sleep.'

Occasionally Alan went to the doorway and
looked out. But always he returned to say that
although the rain had ceased, the darkness
added to the mist and brought visibility down
to no more than two or three feet.

'We shall just have to wait here until they
find us,' Alan said. 'It's no good trying to set
off with the children in these conditions. We
might start walking round in circles, as I did
before I found you.'

They talked quietly, companionably, as
they sat there. Alan asked Lucy about her life
in London then told her a little about the
practice he had joined after qualifying.

'Sylvia, my wife, was a nurse before we
married,' he said. 'We met when I was a
medical student though we did not marry
until I qualified.'

He stared before him, a little smile on his
lips as if the mist and darkness had melted
away and he was looking into the past, a past
that had been full of hope and promise.

'Sylvia was a little older than me,' he said.
'But it made no difference to our love for each
other. I used to think we were the happiest
couple alive. And then when Margy was born
I felt to have everything in life I could ever
want.'

He fell silent and she knew he was thinking

205

of how his happiness had been snatched so cruelly from him by the death of his wife.

'You never married again?' she asked gently.

He shook his head.

'No! I felt I would never be able to find anyone to fill Sylvia's place. Yet sometimes I feel I ought to marry again, if not for my own sake, certainly for Margy's. The child needs a mother.'

There was a sound outside the hut.

'There's a wind rising,' Alan said, a note of excitement in his voice. 'That means that the mist should be blown away.'

They went to the doorway and looked out. Already the mist was thinning. Lucy, looking up, saw a few stars shining through the clouds.

'If the mist goes we might be able to take the children back to Lenthwaite,' she said.

'Yes! I could carry Betty if you could manage Margy,' he said.

They waited. The mist seemed reluctant to go; but the rising wind had the last word.

Soon only long streamers of mist trailed across the moor. The newly risen moon came from behind the clouds and shone down on the moor.

'I can see quite a long way,' Lucy exclaimed; then suddenly her heart missed a beat.

She clutched at Alan's arm and he looked

into her face, startled by her expression.

'What is it, Lucy?' he demanded. 'What have you seen?'

She lifted her hand and pointed a shaking finger across the moor.

There not more than a hundred yards away was the twisted skeleton of the helicopter.

'Mike!' Lucy sobbed and started to run across the rough ground towards the wreckage.


# CHAPTER EIGHTEEN

But Mike was neither in the wrecked helicopter nor on the moor nearby.

'He must have got out alive,' Alan said after they had searched the area around.

'I never heard the crash,' Lucy said, mystified.

'If you were in the hut you probably wouldn't,' Alan said. 'The mist does peculiar things. It can blot sound out very effectively. Besides, I don't think the machine fell very far. It looks more like a stall to me from a few feet above the ground. I certainly didn't hear the crash, but of course I came to the hut from the opposite direction and I wouldn't be likely to notice anything.'

'But where can Mike have got to?' Lucy cried, looking round.

'He probably started off to try and get back to Lenthwaite. Perhaps when we get back ourselves we shall find him already there.'

'Oh, no you won't.'

They both swung round at the sound of the familiar voice.

'Mike!' Lucy cried and ran towards the figure who came swaying from behind the rocks into which the helicopter had almost crashed.

One arm was held across his body. With his free hand he was supporting it under the elbow.

'Sorry I wasn't around when you called,' he said. 'When the mist cleared a bit I thought I'd try and contact someone. But I didn't so came back here to find you two examining the wreckage.'

He looked sadly at the twisted framework of the helicopter.

'How did you get out alive?' Alan asked.

'I was lucky. The door burst open and I was pitchforked out. I landed on my arm. I seem to have broken something.'

'Let me have a look!'

Alan made a quick examination.

'It's the collar bone. You *are* lucky. You might have landed on your head and broken your neck!'

'Serve me right if I had!' Mike said bitterly. 'I don't seem to have been much good in helping to find the missing children.'

Lucy smiled.

'They're safe enough in that hut over there. I found them earlier and Dr. Tolson joined us about two hours ago.'

'Splendid!' he cried, then looking at Lucy with glowing eyes: 'Gosh, but it's good to see you, Lucy! Just for a moment when the rocks loomed up in front of the helicopter I thought I'd bought it.'

'I'd better strap that arm up,' Alan said sharply. 'Have you got a big handkerchief?'

'You can use this scarf,' Lucy said, pulling the silk square from her throat. 'It will make a fairly good sling.'

Presently they walked back to the hut.

'What now?' Mike asked.

'The sooner we get back to Lenthwaite the better,' Alan said, and glancing at Lucy: 'Do you feel like carrying Margy if I carry Betty?'

'Yes, of course! But do you know the way?'

'I daresay we can find it by moonlight.'

Mike laughed. 'Don't worry about that. When I was a boy I spent half my time wandering about these moors. I reckon we're about a mile from town. If you get the children I'll lead the way.'

'Are you sure you feel up to it?' Alan asked. 'You should be suffering from shock as well as from a broken collar-bone.'

'I feel fine!' Mike reassured him. 'Just get the kids and let's be on our way.'

Five minutes later they left the hut behind.

Alan and Lucy, carrying the sleepy children, followed Mike across the trackless moor under the bright light of the moon.

After they had been walking for just over ten minutes a voice hailed them from over on their left.

It was a policeman. His face lit up when he saw the two children.

They explained what had happened and he switched on his walkie-talkie and reported to his superiors. A few moments later he said he'd been told to help them as much as he could on their walk back to Lenthwaite, and, as good as his word, relieved Lucy of her sleeping burden.

Two police cars were waiting at the foot of the track which led up to the moor.

'Goodbye,' Alan said, taking Margy from the policeman and getting into the back of the car. 'I'll see you both later. You'd better get the other police driver to drop Lucy off at home, Mike, then ask him to run you on to the hospital to have that arm set properly.'

'Don't worry! Just get off home and see that Margy gets to bed,' Mike smiled, and slipped his arm about Lucy. 'I'll see to Lucy!'

Just for a moment Alan's eyes met Lucy's, then he looked quickly away, said something to the driver and sat back in his corner, the children beside him.

'He thinks I'm in love with Mike,' Lucy thought in despair. 'If only there was some way of letting him know that he's the one I love. But there isn't, and in any case didn't he tell me that when his wife died he felt he never wanted to marry again?'

She got into the back of the other police car and Mike followed her. On the short ride to her father's house, Mike said:

'You're in love with the doctor, aren't you, Lucy?'

She shook her head angrily.

'I'm not in love with anybody,' she said fiercely, and when he covered her hand with his own she tried to snatch it away. But he held it firmly and made her look into his face. His own was solemn.

'Lucy, I learned something up there on the moor,' he said. 'They say that when you think you're going to die the whole of your life flashes before your eyes. Well, it didn't quite happen to me, but, when the helicopter stalled, and I thought I'd had it, it was Ros I thought of, not you. I know now that she's the one I love, the one I must have loved all along.'

She said nothing, but when the car drew up outside her father's house, she looked at Mike with a smile.

'I'm glad, Mike,' she said quietly. 'I hope you and Rosalind will be very happy.'

He lifted her hand to his lips, then as the police driver opened the door and she got out, he added:

211

'I'm going to propose to her as soon as I reach home.'

As the driver prepared to drive away he said:

'No hard feelings, then, Lucy?'

She shook her head.

'I never did love you, Mike,' she said. 'I think you must have guessed that from the start.'

Ruefully he nodded. 'I suppose you're right but—well, I just wouldn't admit the fact to myself.'

She watched the car drive down the street and out into the main road, then, with a sigh, she turned and went into the house.

## CHAPTER NINETEEN

The two young people looked at Sister hopefully. She smiled.

'It will only have to be for a few minutes,' she said. 'Your father's still a very sick man, Mr. Earnshaw, though the doctor says he's definitely over the worst.'

Mike looked down at the girl by his side.

'Perhaps you'd better wait out here, Ros,' he said; but she shook her head.

'No, I'm coming in with you, Mike. He mightn't believe you if I'm not by your side.'

'Very well!'

Hand in hand they followed Sister into the Intensive Care Unit. The patient was lying with closed eyes. A nurse was sitting by his side, her eyes on the battery of instruments beside her which were monitoring her patient's condition.

At a nod from Sister she stood up and went into the outer room.

'Just three or four minutes,' Sister warned in a low voice, then bending over her patient: 'Mr. Earnshaw, you have visitors.'

Slowly the heavy eyes opened. The mill owner looked up and saw the young couple by his bedside.

'Why, Mike! And you—Rosalind!' he muttered, and with a frown seeing his son's arm in a sling: 'But you're hurt, Mike!'

'It's nothing, Dad! Just a broken collar-bone.' His eyes shone as he looked down at his father. 'Dad, we have some news for you! Ros has promised to marry me!'

The sick man frowned as if the news was too much for him to take in. Then a delighted smile spread over his pale drawn face.

'You—you mean?—'

A tear rolled slowly down his face. Ros bent to kiss him.

'Now the two businesses will become one,' she whispered, 'just as you've always wanted.'

'God bless you, child!' He held out his hand to Mike. 'I've done a lot of thinking as I've lain here, Mike. I decided that if I was spared I'd pass the business over to you. Oh, I realise now that I've not been fair to you in the past. But that's all over now. With Rosalind by your side you'll make a go of it, I'm sure. Your mother and I will be proud of you yet.'

Mike glanced at Rosalind.

'We'll do our best, won't we, Ros?' he said, then seeing Sister hovering in the doorway: 'We must go now, Dad. Hurry up and get better. Even if we run the two firms as one, we'll need lots of advice from you.'

They turned away and the sick man's gaze followed them until they disappeared. There was a new light in his eyes, a light of hope and determination to get well.

'Maybe I'll live to see my grandson born,' he thought, 'and then the firm of Earnshaw and Murgatroyd will go on and on into the distant future.'

Although it was Alan's day at the mill he had not turned up by half past ten the following morning.

There were several workpeople waiting outside the First Aid department door and when Lucy decided that Alan could not be attending the mill, she sent the people away with instructions to return in the afternoon.

At eleven o'clock the phone rang. It was Alan. He sounded worried.

'I'm afraid I shan't be coming in today, Lucy,' he said. 'I've been up most of the night with Margy. She caught a cold up on the moor yesterday and I don't like the look of her. Her mother suffered from bronchitis and Margy takes after her, I'm afraid. At any rate I've asked Dr. Wadsworth to call this morning and I want to be there when he comes.'

'I do hope she'll improve,' Lucy said.

'Thanks!' he said then rather abruptly rang off.

She spent the rest of the morning wishing she could go to the house and see the child for herself, but she felt that Alan would not welcome that.

She realised that she must possess herself in patience. No doubt Alan would ring again when he had more news.

But the phone remained silent. In the afternoon she telephoned the house. Mrs. Barrett answered.

'The doctor's out,' she said. 'He had to go out on his rounds.'

'How's Margy?' Lucy asked.

'Much better, I'm glad to say! She says she wants to get up!'

Lucy's heart rose.

'Tell Dr. Tolson I rang,' Lucy said, and because there was little else she could say, she replaced the receiver.

When she got home that evening she found Bessie and Dick with her mother and father. They turned happy faces towards her as she

215

went into the kitchen.

Lucy saw that Bessie's eyes were shining and that Dick was standing with his arm about her shoulders.

'Oh, Lucy, we're getting married,' Bessie burst out. 'Dick came to see me when I left the office. He wanted to tell me about Mr. Mike and Miss Murgatroyd, though of course I already knew. Mr. Mike told me earlier.'

She gave a happy little laugh. 'He said that as marriage was in the air why shouldn't we get engaged as well?'

'Better late than never,' Mrs. Hirst said. 'It's taken our Dick a long time to get round to it but he's finally made it!'

Lucy kissed her friend.

'I'm so happy for you both!' she cried. 'Will you stay on at Murgatroyd's as manager, Dick?'

'I don't know,' he replied. 'It depends what happens when Mike and Ros get married. But there'll be a place for me in one firm or the other, I'm sure of that.'

Later Lucy went up to her bedroom. She wanted to be alone. Suddenly she felt very unhappy.

First Mike and Rosalind—now Dick and Bessie.

She was the only one who didn't seem able to achieve real happiness.

She heard a car draw up outside the house. Going to the window she looked out into the street.

Below she saw Alan Tolson making across the pavement. As he knocked at the door she put her hand to her breast to still the sudden thundering of her heart.

'Lucy! Lucy!' It was Dick's voice. 'Dr. Tolson wants a word with you.'

She looked into the mirror. Her hair was a mess. She hadn't had time to make up her face since she arrived home.

Then she told herself not to be a fool. Why should she worry what she looked like? She meant nothing to Alan.

He was waiting in the passage. Dick had disappeared so she took him into the little-used sitting room. It felt chill and stuffy.

'Lucy, it's Margy,' he said.

She stared at him, suddenly alarmed.

'Margy! Is—is she worse?'

He shook his head. He was smiling now, a smile which lit up his grey eyes.

'Far from it,' he said. 'She's much better this evening. But she insists on seeing "Nursie", as she calls you.'

She smiled back at him delighted at the news.

'Would you like me to go with you?' she asked.

He nodded. 'If you could spare the time. It would make her very happy.'

'I'll just get my coat!'

As she turned to the door he said in a low voice:

'There's a rumour in the town that Mike Earnshaw has got engaged. One of my patients said she'd heard something of the sort.'

She looked back at him.

'It's true,' she said.

He avoided her eyes.

'I hope you'll both be very happy,' he said quietly.

She frowned. What did he mean? Then suddenly she knew!

'But he's not asked me to marry him!' she cried. 'He's got engaged to Rosalind Murgatroyd!'

He stared at her unable to believe his ears. Then his face lit up.

'You—you mean you're not marrying him? But I thought—'

She laughed.

'Mike never loved me, neither did I ever love him!' she said. 'A lot of people seem to have got the wrong ideas about us.'

He went towards her. His hand came out for hers.

'Lucy, I can hardly take this in,' he said. 'All I know is that you're free.'

Gently she drew her hand out of his and made for the door.

'I'll get my coat,' she said and went from the room.

When she returned he was standing by the window looking out into the street.

Slowly he turned back to her.

'Lucy, let's go to Margy,' he said quietly. 'Later I'll put a question to you. I only hope your answer will be yes.'

They left the room together. Lucy went to the kitchen door and looked in at the four expectant faces turned towards her.

'I'm going to Dr. Tolson's to see his little daughter who's ill,' she said, then with a smile: 'When I come back I may have some news for you.'

Before anyone could speak she closed the door; then she made along the narrow passage to the front door where Alan was waiting.

Photoset, printed and bound in Great Britain by REDWOOD PRESS LIMITED, Melksham, Wiltshire